HOME-FRONT HEROES

"In a small Georgia town during World War II, Kate Coleman and her sixth-grade classmates move into a primitive shack while new classrooms are built. With good spirit, the children accept the inconvenience as well as other homefront hardships such as food shortages, gas rationing, and separation from loved ones. . . . The evocation of the 1940s and the vivid, rural Georgia background make this a pleasant trip back in time."
—*Library Journal*

"Burch has written a gentle, leisurely story. . . . [He] believes in the elasticity of children. The war may sometimes dampen Kate's spirits, but she will cope. As in his *Queenie Peavy*, the author has created another lively, independent girl character [in Kate Coleman]."
—*The New York Times Book Review*

HOME-FRONT HEROES

Robert Burch

Illustrated by Ronald Himler

PUFFIN BOOKS

PUFFIN BOOKS
Published by the Penguin Group
Viking Penguin, a division of Penguin Books USA Inc.,
375 Hudson Street, New York, New York 10014, U.S.A.
Penguin Books Ltd, 27 Wrights Lane, London W8 5TZ, England
Penguin Books Australia Ltd, Ringwood, Victoria, Australia
Penguin Books Canada Ltd, 10 Alcorn Avenue, Toronto, Ontario, Canada M4V 3B2
Penguin Books (N.Z.) Ltd, 182–190 Wairau Road, Auckland 10, New Zealand

Penguin Books Ltd, Registered Offices: Harmondsworth, Middlesex, England

First published in the United States of America
as *Hut School and the Wartime Homefront Heroes*
by The Viking Press, 1974
Published in Puffin Books, 1992
1   3   5   7   9   10   8   6   4   2
Copyright © Robert Burch, 1974
All rights reserved

LIBRARY OF CONGRESS CATALOGING-IN-PUBLICATION DATA
Burch, Robert, 1925–
[Hut School and the wartime home-front heroes]
Homefront heroes / by Robert Burch.   p.   cm.
Originally published: Hut School and the wartime home-front
heroes. 1st ed. New York : Viking Press, 1974.
Summary: Describes the impact of World War II on a sixth grade
class in Georgia.
ISBN 0-14-036030-1 (pbk.)
[1. Schools—Fiction.   2. World War, 1939–1945—United States—
Fiction.]   I. Title.
PZ7.B91585Ho   1992   [Fic]—dc20   91-31426

Printed in the United States of America
Set in Fairfield Medium

For my brother Ambrose

Contents

"Don't Get Rid of Gooney While I'm Gone"

KATE COLEMAN had climbed Stone Mountain. She had done a lot of exciting things in her life. She had been swimming in Mirror Lake and drunk water from Indian Springs. She had fired a pistol, a rifle, and a shotgun in the Flint River swamp. She had ridden the escalator at Rich's, a department store in Atlanta, and she had been to a picture show at the Fox Theater, where the lights in the ceiling twinkled like stars. She had spent a day at the Southeastern Fair and stayed until after dark for the fireworks. She had seen inside an airplane, but she had not ridden in one. Except for that, Kate guessed she had done just about everything there was to do in the part of Georgia in which she lived. And it was a good thing, because there was a war on now, World War II, and sometimes she felt as if she had never been away from Redhill. Gas was rationed, and so were tires. War was an inconvenience.

"I think I'll go around the world," she told her father. They were waiting at the dining-room table for breakfast.

"Will you leave this morning?" he asked.

"I don't know, but I'm quitting school today for sure."

Her mother called from the kitchen, "It only started Monday."

"I know," answered Kate. "But I'm tired of it."

"Then you definitely should quit," said her father. "I hated the sixth grade myself."

Kate smiled. "Did you really?"

"The fourth grade was even worse. My schooling almost ended that year on account of long division. I still don't see much excuse for arithmetic!"

"Me, either," said Kate.

"Then let's do away with it," he said. "Add it to the list."

Kate brought out a sheet of tablet paper from the sideboard drawer. On it was listed what she and her father planned to abolish if either of them ever ruled the world. "How do you spell arithmetic?" she asked.

"*M-a-t-h*," said Mr. Coleman, and Kate added it to the list that already contained buttermilk, mosquitoes, rain on Saturdays, and a variety of other things for which she and her father felt there was no real need. The list ran heavily to foods they did not like, possibly because they kept it in the dining room and were more apt to think about it at mealtime. "I believe I'll add hats too," said Kate. "Is that all right with you?"

"Sure," said her father. "Make it, *Hats, yellow or otherwise.*"

An aunt had sent Kate a yellow hat on her birthday. Mrs. Coleman had insisted that it was just right for Kate, setting off her black hair and green eyes, and that it should be worn to church some Sunday. But Kate had no intention of wearing it. "I may abolish that one by dropping it in an ocean!" she said.

"What will be the first stop on your journey?" asked Mr. Coleman.

"Africa," said Kate. "I plan to catch an elephant and a lion and a few other animals, and then move on to India and trap a tiger or two. After that, I'll gather up a bunch of monkeys, and then I'll bring everything home and start a zoo. Would you care to help run it?"

"I'll resign my job today so that I can be your zoo keeper."

Mrs. Coleman brought a bowl of scrambled eggs to the table. "You both need a keeper!" she said.

"You never take us seriously," said Mr. Coleman. "But you're going to be surprised one morning when you wake up and discover there's a zebra on your doorstep!"

Kate laughed. "And an elephant on the lawn and a giraffe looking in the window!"

Her father added, "And monkeys shelling peanuts on the living-room rug!" He and Kate laughed uproariously, and Mrs. Coleman smiled as she returned to the kitchen. Mr. Coleman called to her, "I may just travel with Kate. Could you manage without me for a while?"

"Oh, sure," said Mrs. Coleman, coming back into the dining room with a platter of toast. "Who needs you anyway?" She smiled at him as she took her place at the table. "Now have some toast," she said, "and pass the eggs to Kate, and let's talk sensible for a while. I couldn't sleep last night for thinking about the boys at the depot yesterday." She had gone with Sara Hatfield, a neighbor, to the railway station to a program honoring the young men who were being drafted into military service. Sara's cousin had been among them. Twice a month, when the county's draftees caught the train, there was a short farewell program for them. Mr. Logan, the chairman of the draft board, always made a few comments, and a preacher from one of the churches of the area would say a prayer, and everyone would wave as the train pulled out of the station. It carried the men to Fort McPherson in Atlanta, where they were kept for a few days and then sent to training camps around the country.

Mrs. Coleman continued, "Mr. Logan told the crowd how brave the men were to be going off to defend our glorious nation and how he looked forward to the day we would all be assembled to greet them home from war instead of sending them off to it."

"That's what he always says," said Mr. Coleman. "I've been to some of those ceremonies."

Mrs. Coleman said, "What got me was how happy everyone pretended to be."

"What'd you expect them to do, weep and moan?"

"No, but it's a front to pretend that the war's a big lark."

"We all have to put up a front at times."

"Some of the men were my and your age, but a lot of them looked like kids."

"They were at least eighteen," said Kate. "You have to be at least eighteen to get drafted."

"I know," said her mother, "but some of them were boyish-looking even for eighteen. And no one acted as if there were any doubt that every last one of the men getting on the train would come home eventually. But some of them won't ever come back!" Her voice almost broke as she added, "Some of them will be killed."

"Of course they will," said Mr. Coleman. "But you didn't expect Mr. Logan to say, 'Well, now, gentlemen, some of you ain't never coming back, do you hear?'" Sounding as if he were giving a speech, he continued, "Some of you are gonna get your guts shot out, and you'll die a long way from home—so a special good-by to you this morning. And to the rest of you, well, maybe we'll be here when you come back, and maybe we won't. It all depends on how busy we are at other things by then."

"No, I didn't say he should have said that. I don't really know what he should have said; maybe just exactly what he did say. But still I can't get over the way it was. Why, you'd have thought the draftees were off to the grandest party that had ever been given. I saw wives and mothers blinking back tears, but the fathers and brothers and friends were shouting as if the occasion were the grandest thing! And the men who were leaving were shouting and laughing, too. 'We'll tree ol' Hitler like a possum' one boy yelled, and another said, 'Yeah, we'll chase him up a 'simmon tree and bring him home in a gunnysack.' But there was one little thin-faced boy who didn't yell or look as if he were enjoying any of it. Just as the train was leaving he stuck his head out the window and called to his father, 'Now don't get rid of Gooney while I'm gone!'"

"What'd his father say?" asked Kate.

"Nothing," said Mrs. Coleman. "He cut himself a plug of chewing tobacco and acted as if he hadn't heard. I thought about that boy in the night and wondered if he was lying awake in the barracks, feeling all alone."

"All alone!" said Kate. "A barracks is full of soldiers!"

"He could still feel all alone," said Mr. Coleman. "The bigger the crowd, the more alone I feel sometimes."

"Then you're *not* cut out for the army," said Mrs. Coleman, as if someone had said that he was. She went back to talking about the thin-faced boy. "I wonder who Gooney is. It could be his dog . . . or it could be a mule that won't be needed now that he's not home to plow it . . . or it could be a cow."

15

"Probably it's his mother," said Mr. Coleman, and he and Kate laughed.

"Oh, you turn everything into a joke," said Mrs. Coleman.

"I'm going into service when I grow up," said Kate. "In England girls get to drive ambulances. Do you think the Marines would let me drive an ambulance for them?"

"They'd be glad to have you," said Mr. Coleman.

"Good!" said Kate. "I hope the war lasts till I can get in it."

"No, Kate," said her mother, "you don't wish that."

The war had lasted almost two years already. At least, the United States had been in it that long. Some countries had been fighting longer, but the United States had not started until the Japanese attacked Pearl Harbor. That was on December 7, 1941, and Kate could remember the day as clearly as if it had been no more than a week ago. It had been a Sunday, and she and Dudley Shaw, from next door, had been shooting marbles in his backyard when Mrs. Shaw called, "Quick, Kate, run tell your folks to turn on the radio!" Partly because Mrs. Shaw had sounded alarmed, and partly because it was Dudley's shot and if he made it good he would win the game, Kate had hurried inside with the message.

Her parents spent the rest of the day listening to news reports, stopping at times to explain to Kate, as best they could, what it all meant. The country had been drawn into World War II. In answer to her questions, they said that no, they didn't believe any of the fighting would be in the United States; American troops would be scattered around the world instead. As to how long the war would last, no one knew.

Later in the afternoon Kate went back outside. Dudley came out, and they talked about the war and whom they knew who might be in it. Their classmate, Louise Lockwood, had a brother in the Navy, but the Lockwoods lived out in the country, and Dudley and Kate did not know Louise's family very well. Also, there was Marcus Holbrook, Ivy's brother. He had been in the Army before the Holbrooks moved to Redhill, but he had been in town for two weeks last summer. Kate knew of nobody else in military service, and she did not believe anyone really close to her would be drafted. She had no brothers or uncles, and surely her father would be left at home to look after her mother and herself. So she and Dudley went back to the marbles that were just as they had left them. He made his shot good, winning that game, but Kate won the next three in a row, and by then it was suppertime.

Mr. Coleman was so serious all evening that Kate worried about him instead of a war that was far from home. He had always noticed a funny side to whatever happened, but even he did not make jokes about Pearl Harbor.

Gradually the Colemans, along with families all over the United States, became accustomed to the war. There were sacrifices that people on the home front were called on to make, and rationing became a part of daily life. Shoes were rationed, and so were certain foods, including meat and sugar. Some things that were not rationed were scarce—or missing for "the duration," which had come to mean the duration of the war.

There were other shortages too—such as the gas one. But Kate stopped complaining that she and her parents did not get to go places the way they once did. Her father needed the family's gasoline allotment in getting to and from his job with the insurance firm in Decatur. If he couldn't commute to work, he would have to stay up there, coming home only on weekends, and she could not imagine going a whole week without seeing her father.

Kate took the spoon from the bowl that had contained the

scrambled eggs and licked it. "All right," she said, "I take it back. I don't hope the war lasts till I can get in it."

"I wish it would end today!" said Mrs. Coleman.

Mr. Coleman smiled. "Meanwhile, Kate and I have declared our own private war on certain things."

"What things?" asked Mrs. Coleman.

"Oh, scalloped potatoes, oatmeal, stewed prunes, and any number of dishes you insist on serving us just because they're healthy. Why can't we have chocolate cake instead?"

"Because there's a war on!" said Mrs. Coleman. "Sugar's rationed, didn't you know? But I'll save our quota, and maybe we'll have enough for a cake by the end of the month. But it won't be chocolate. There's a shortage of that too."

Just then there was a knock on the door. Kate jumped up. "Coming, Dudley!" she called, without opening the door to see who was there. She grabbed her books and explained, "I'm going to race him to the schoolhouse," as if she and Dudley didn't race each other every time they went anywhere.

"I thought you were quitting school," teased Mr. Coleman.

"I'll give it another chance," said Kate. "But I wish Miss Jordan wouldn't treat us like babies," she complained as she went out the door. "You'd think we were first graders."

All the
Boys and Kate

"ON YOUR HEAD!" said Miss Jordan. "Quick now, everybody, stand on your head!"

Nobody moved.

"Then jump up and down!" she said. At that she jumped up and down, but nobody else did. Rapidly she gave other commands: "Wave your right hand in the air! Kick out your left foot! Stand on your toes!"

Still nobody moved.

"Sit down!" she said, flopping to the ground. Out of breath she said, "Simon says, 'Sit down.'"

All the sixth graders sat down except Nola May Foster, who never could remember that you were supposed to do what Simon said.

"Nola May's out!" said Sylvia Gage.

"Yes, I see," said Miss Jordan. "But let's rest a minute. Let's just sit here and watch the train come in." The station was across the street from the end of the schoolyard, and the train to Atlanta was arriving. The students began talking with each other while they watched it.

Kate whispered to Tootie Poe, "Simon says sixth graders are too big to play Simon Says!" Tootie was one of Kate's best friends, although they seldom saw each other except in school. Tootie and her twin brother, Zack, like many of the students, lived in the country. Sometimes Kate envied them their riding the bus, but at the same time she couldn't imagine living anywhere except in town and being able to walk—or run—to school.

Tootie laughed, her brown eyes sparkling. "Yeah," she said. "Simon says Miss Jordan must think we're little kids. But I like her anyway."

"I suppose I do too," said Kate. School had only been in session four days, and that wasn't long enough to really know how she felt about the new teacher. Still she had to admit that except for treating her students as if they were younger than they were, Miss Jordan was nice. And she was young and pretty—there was no doubt about that.

Alex Bronson, whose father was principal of the grammar school, had told Kate that Miss Jordan had been hired to teach the first grade in Redhill. "Ol' Mrs. Hanks quit," he reported, "and Miss Jordan was to take her place. But nobody could be found to teach sixth grade, and with the war on and all, Dad tried to talk Mrs. Hanks into teaching us, but she wouldn't do it. She said she'd take the first grade back instead, and that's how we got Miss Jordan."

Tootie whispered to Kate, "What if we had Miss Dillman for our teacher?" and both of them made a face. Miss Dillman taught the seventh grade, and the first day of school the sixth and seventh grades had taken their morning recess together. Miss Dillman had ruined it by screaming at the students about what they couldn't do. "You cannot, I said, *cannot* play on this side of the building!" she had yelled. "The other grades are at work." Everyone had moved to the opposite side, and away from the building, for a game of ball. Then someone had cheered when a home run was made, and Miss Dillman had screamed, "You cannot yell, even if we are at the far end of the playground. Sound carries!" She had made more noise than anybody. The next day the sixth grade was assigned a different time for recess, and Kate was glad of it. It was fun to be outside with just Miss Jordan, even if today they had wound up playing Simon Says.

The train was in the station by now, and a group of men began to board it. Miss Jordan, who was as new to Redhill as she was to teaching, asked, "Why are so many people catching the train this morning?"

"This is draft day," said Dudley.

"But didn't the men who were being drafted leave yesterday?"

"The ones yesterday went to stay," explained Dudley. "The ones today are going to take tests to see if the Army wants them. Then they can come home for three weeks before they have to go back."

"Unless they go in the Navy," said Alex. "Then they don't get but a week."

Ivy Holbrook said, "Miss Jordan, my brother's in the war."

"We know," said Oscar Yates. "He's not the only one!" Ivy was always talking about her brother, who was in the Army. "And before that, he was a football star. You've told us before."

Henry Inman said, "Someday I'm gonna join the Navy."

"I may get in it right away!" said Zack Poe, Tootie's twin brother, and everybody laughed. Zack was always saying that he was a man instead of a boy. He and his sister, both of whom were dark and strikingly handsome, were the age of their classmates, but Zack was bigger than the other boys, and he looked older. It ran in the family. Brewster, an older brother, had enlisted in the Navy at fifteen and was halfway through boot camp when it was discovered that he had lied about his age. Some people said the Navy might have kept him if Mr. Poe hadn't raised such a ruckus. Mr. Poe was reported to have said that he needed Brewster to help run the farm and that if he wasn't sent home in a hurry the Navy would have more than one war on its hands. Kate didn't doubt it; Tootie had told her about Mr. Poe's terrible temper.

"All right," said Miss Jordan, getting up, "we've rested long enough. On your feet, everybody!"

Everyone got up but Kate. Miss Jordan asked, "Don't you feel well?"

"Yes, ma'am, I feel fine."

"Then why aren't you standing?"

"Simon didn't say, 'On your feet!' " said Kate.

Miss Jordan laughed. "Why, so he didn't! I guess that means everybody's out but you, which makes it your turn to be Simon."

Kate went to the front of the group. "Let me think," she said, just as the train blew its whistle and pulled out of the station. It moved slowly along the track directly across from the schoolyard. "Oh, yes," she said. "Wave at Mr. Wilson." Everyone knew Mr. Wilson. He was the conductor on the train, the only passenger one to come through Redhill. It went to Atlanta every morning and returned in late afternoon. Kate waved, and so did Nola May Foster.

"Nola May's out!" said Sylvia Gage, and Nola May stepped over to the side. Kate was more interested in the train than Simon Says, but when she realized that no one else was waving, she said quickly, "Simon says, 'Everybody wave at Mr. Wilson.' "

All the sixth graders and Miss Jordan began waving, and Mr.

Wilson waved back at them. The men on the train who were being drafted began waving, too, and when they saw Miss Jordan, two of them gave loud whistles, or wolf calls. Other draftees piled onto the observation platform of the last car, shouting and waving. One of them, wearing overalls and a wide-brim straw hat, called to Miss Jordan, "You look just like a moving-picture star!" and another yelled, "Come with us to Fort McPherson!" They were all laughing and waving, and so were Miss Jordan and the boys and girls, as the train gained speed and went out of sight. Then Kate said, "All right, back to the game! Simon says, 'On your mark, everybody, as if you were about to run a race.'"

Crouching along with everyone else, she looked over at Alex Bronson and grinned. The two of them and Dudley were always racing each other. They claimed to be the fastest runners in school. Then Kate said, "Simon says, 'Everybody run and hide and don't come back till lunchtime!'"

Immediately all the boys and Kate raced across the schoolyard. Some ran into a clump of chinaberry trees, some rounded the corner of the building, and others disappeared down the boiler-room steps. The girls, except for Kate, stood where they were and laughed.

"*Boys!*" called Miss Jordan. "Come back! This is only recess!" But none of them returned. Kate, Alex, and Dudley doubled back, stooping as they ran. A low hedge that bordered one side of the school ground kept them from being seen. Soon they were only a few yards from where they had started, listening to Miss Jordan say, "What on earth got into those boys that they would do a thing like that?"

"It's not just the boys," said Sylvia, adjusting the clip that held back her long, blonde curls. "Kate Coleman is with them."

Kate whispered, "That stupid Sylvia!"

"Well, we've got to get them back without disturbing the whole school," said Miss Jordan. "The other grades are having lessons, and we're not supposed to play near the building. I can't scream at them so—"

Sylvia interrupted her. "Here comes Mr. Bronson. Maybe he can help us."

Miss Jordan put her hand to her forehead. "Oh, no, let's don't ask him to help us with a little thing like this. We may already be in trouble about yesterday." The previous day the class had taken a trash can onto the playground to use as third base in a ball game. No one had known there was a rule against it, but Miss Dillman had reported them. The day before that, she had reported them for accidentally breaking a scrubby little boxwood that had been planted by the Redhill Garden Club. The boxwood had been second base. Today Miss Jordan had decided they wouldn't play ball; they'd play Simon Says.

"Good morning," said Mr. Bronson, and Miss Jordan smiled at him. "Something has come up," he continued, "and I need to discuss it with you inside. Do you think your students could play by themselves for the rest of their recess period?"

Miss Jordan said, "Why, yes, I believe they could." She turned to the girls and said, "Simon says, 'Go find all the boys and tell them to line up quietly and return to our room.' Recess is almost over."

"Yes, ma'am," said the girls—all except Sylvia Gage. She remained at Miss Jordan's side instead of running across the playground. "What about Kate Coleman? She ran away too."

Miss Jordan looked as if she wished Sylvia Gage had run away. But she patted her on the head and gave her a little shove in the direction of the chinaberry trees. "Simon says, 'Go find all the boys and Kate.'" Then she and Mr. Bronson went toward his office.

The News

"SIT DOWN and shut up!" screamed Miss Dillman. "Do you hear me? I said sit down and shut up!"

The sixth graders had returned to their room after recess when Kate and the boys had decided against trying to stay hidden till lunchtime, but Miss Jordan was still in Mr. Bronson's office. They had stayed quiet at first. But when Tubby Elrod threw the spelling book at Henry Inman, they'd become a bit noisy. The book would not have hit Winnie Owens on the head if she hadn't stood up just at that moment. Even so, it didn't hurt her, and she threw it back at Tubby, hitting Melvin Attaway on the shoulder. Melvin had the book, and everyone was standing to see what he would do with it when Miss Dillman came across the hall from the seventh grade. "Now if I hear one more sound out of you," she said, "you're all going to Mr. Bronson."

"Me, too?" asked Alex Bronson, and his classmates snickered.

"Now sit down and shut up!" said Miss Dillman again. She turned and left the room.

Everyone stayed quiet until Miss Jordan returned a few moments later. "I have the most exciting news," she said, sitting down on top of her desk and pulling her feet under her. "The school has overflowed!"

"Where?" asked Henry Inman, standing up and looking out the window. "I don't see any water."

Miss Jordan laughed. "It's not that kind of overflowing," she said. "What's happened is that we'll have too many pupils in the school for the building to hold everyone. Children whose parents work at the Ordnance Depot will be coming here."

Kate had heard her father talk about the big Ordnance Depot. He went past it on his way to work, and she had heard him speak of it as being "just over the county line." Oscar Yates must have heard someone describe it in the same way because he said, "The Ordnance Depot is not in our county."

"No, but a number of the people who work there are moving into a temporary housing complex that's in this county, and some of the children—seventy in all—will come to school here."

Alice King asked, "Will any of them be in our room?"

"No, only the first through fourth graders are coming to Redhill. Arrangements have been made with other school systems to take the older boys and girls. Two new rooms will be added to our building right away—one for a combination first and second grade, and one for a third and fourth. But the children arrive Monday, and guess what? In order to provide space for them, we'll be one of the two grades to give up our room!"

"Yipee!" said Dudley, standing up. "No more school!"

"May we leave now?" asked Kate, heading for the door. She called to Dudley, "I'll race you to the corner."

"Sit down! Sit down!" said Miss Jordan just as Miss Dillman came into the room.

26

"Oh!" said Miss Dillman when she saw Miss Jordan. "I didn't know you were back. I was coming to quiet your room."

"We'll be a little quieter now," promised Miss Jordan; and everyone sat down as Miss Dillman gave them a disgusted look before stalking out.

Miss Jordan smiled at her students. "You really must help me keep order," she said. "In college I trained with younger children, and you're so much bigger than they were that I don't always know what to do. But you'll help me, won't you?"

"Oh, yes, ma'am," said Alvin Attaway. "We'll help you."

Zack Poe stepped to the front of the room. "I'll take charge," he said. "Don't worry about it." Then he turned to the class and said, "All right, you guys, shut your traps! Do you hear?"

Everybody laughed, including Zack and Miss Jordan, as he went back to his seat.

"Now about the exciting news," continued Miss Jordan. "New rooms are to be added, as I've said, but it may be two months before they're ready."

"Yipee!" said Dudley. "No school for two months!"

"Nothing of the sort!" said Miss Jordan. "But wouldn't it be fun if that were true! What would you do with two more months of vacation, Dudley?"

"I'd play ball and go swimming every day."

"I'd go fishing," said Zack. "I'd seine for crawfish and I'd use their tails for bait and I'd catch a five-pound bass every day—maybe two or three."

"Aw, you didn't catch a big fish all summer," said Tootie.

"Why, I did!" said Zack. "I caught lots of big fish. I just never did bring them home."

"All right," said Miss Jordan, "let's not argue." Then she looked at Nola May, who was waving her hand. "Yes, Nola May?"

"If I had two more weeks—I mean, months—of vacation, I'd crochet me a dress. I already learnt how to crochet."

"I *have* already *learned* how to crochet," corrected Miss Jordan. "And that's very nice. What color would you make it?"

"I'd have to decide," said Nola May; and Dinah Myrtle Moore said, "I'd make a yellow one. One of my boyfriends likes yellow." Some of the students snickered. Dinah Myrtle was three years older than most of them, and she brought up the subject of her boyfriends every chance she had.

Alice King said, "I think a red dress with a pale blue band around the edges would be pretty."

Hope Nelson sighed as if the thought of such a beautiful dress was more than she could stand. She always thought Alice's ideas were wonderful. "Alice is going to be a fashion designer when she grows up."

"That should be an interesting field," said Miss Jordan.

Ivy Holbrook spoke up. "I wrote my brother to send me a dress like those women over there wear, and he said they didn't wear dresses."

"You mean they go around naked?" asked Henry.

"No," said Ivy. "They wear sarongs. And I wrote him then to send me one of them. He's on an island in the South Pacific."

Oscar Yates said disgustedly, "You'd think Ivy's brother was the only person from around here in the war, but he ain't."

"He *isn't*," corrected Miss Jordan. "And no, I agree that he isn't, but at the same time I know how Ivy feels." Kate noticed that Miss Jordan's smile vanished briefly and she looked as if she were thinking of something far away.

Ivy continued, "He said he might."

"Might what?" asked Miss Jordan.

"Send me a sarong. Can I wear it to school if he does?"

"*May* I wear it to school? And, yes, I think that would be lovely. I don't know how Mr. Bronson and Miss Dillman and the other teachers would feel about it, but I think it would be nice. Everybody in favor of Ivy wearing her sarong to school, raise your hands."

Every hand in the room went up, including Miss Jordan's. "There," she said, "that's settled, and now it's my turn to talk again." She tapped her desk with a lipstick. "Can all of you see those two big houses across the street?" Her students stood up and looked out the window, although the houses had been there for many years. Both were two-story homes with big yards in front and back. At some distance in the rear, at the edge of woods, were two smaller houses that looked as if they had once been servants' quarters.

Glenn Rigby pointed at one of the big houses. "I live in that one," he said, "and the Patersons live in the other one."

"That's right," said Miss Jordan. "And did you know that your father and Mr. Paterson have offered the two little houses down by the woods for the school to use until our new rooms are ready?"

Dudley said, "But we use the Patersons' cabin for a scout hut."

"I suppose it's been decided that the scouts want to share their meeting place with the school. Mr. Paterson is on the Board of Education." She smiled as if she could persuade her students to be happy if she appeared cheerful enough, but everyone was frowning.

"And ours is full of garden tools and old furniture and stuff," said Glenn.

"It's to be cleaned out," said Miss Jordan. "Isn't it generous of your father and Mr. Paterson to offer us the cabins? And the

29

School Board has decided to move two grades down there temporarily, and they think we're big enough to be one of them. Aren't we complimented?"

No one looked the least bit complimented.

"What other grade is going?" asked Sylvia.

"The fifth, I believe."

Kate thought, Well, at least we'll get away from Miss Dillman! She had been afraid that the seventh grade would be the other one to move since it was the top class in grammar school. High school, five blocks away, started with the eighth grade.

Everyone was frowning until Kate said, "Miss Jordan, I think it's a good idea." At that, her classmates began saying yes, they thought it was a good idea too. Kate added, "Maybe there are some wild animals down there we can capture."

"I'm glad you're pleased," said Miss Jordan. "But, no, there are not apt to be any wild animals, are there, Glenn?"

"Yes, ma'am," said Glenn. "Somebody trapped a bobcat down there not long ago."

"Well, maybe it was the only one in the woods. And now that it's been caught, there's really nothing to worry about." She was the only one who looked as if a bobcat were anything to worry about.

"There are some snakes too," said Glenn. "I've killed a heap of snakes down there."

"You don't mean it?" said Miss Jordan, sounding alarmed.

"But not all of them were deadly," added Glenn.

Zack Poe said, "Don't worry, Miss Jordan, I'll protect you from snakes." He stood up and swung his arms as if he were killing a snake with a long stick. "Blam!" he said. "Take that! And take that! Blam! Blam!" He jumped about, pretending that he was swatting at a snake. When his demonstration ended, he said, "And anyway snakes'll go underground or somewhere when cold weather gets here."

"I hope we won't be there when cold weather arrives," said Miss Jordan. In the part of Georgia where Redhill was located, mild weather usually continued until late in the fall. "And I hope there's nothing else down there to threaten us." Hesitantly she asked, "Is there, Glenn?"

"No, ma'am," he answered; and Miss Jordan looked relieved until Kate said, "How about quicksand, Glenn? You told me once there was a strip of quicksand down there."

"I made that up," confessed Glenn. "But there's lots of poison ivy."

Miss Jordan looked worried, but her students smiled as if they could persuade her to be happy if they appeared cheerful enough.

Wartime
Saturday

"Hooray!" said Kate. "The end of the string beans!" She held up a half-filled market basket.

Mr. Coleman, toting a sprinkling can across the end of the garden, asked, "Are those really the last ones?"

"There's not a bean left," said Kate. "Ain't that nice?"

"It sure is!" said her father. "I'm tired of them, too. But your mother's been canning all that we haven't eaten, so I'm afraid she'll keep serving them to us!"

Kate walked down a row of holes that her father had dug. It was hard to imagine that one of the spindly plants that he was putting into them would grow into a head of cabbage by next spring or summer. "I like sauerkraut," she said. "And cole slaw is pretty good. But cooked cabbage, yuk!"

"Maybe we should bargain with your mother," said Mr. Coleman, "and insist that our crop be used for kraut or slaw only. Let's tell her that otherwise we'll plow up our victory garden!"

Because of the war, people all over the country had been urged to grow as much of their own food as possible. Most families in Redhill had always grown their vegetables, but Kate and her father had been new at gardening until last year. Mr. Coleman, who had been reared in the city, said that Kate knew as much about growing things as he did, and Kate realized that he was right. But together they had learned, and together they were proud of all they had grown—even if this year they had produced more beans than they wanted to eat. "We've been lucky on everything but the late corn," said Kate, slapping at a bedraggled stalk. "Grow!" she said. "There's a war on, and you're needed!"

"Oh, well," said Mr. Coleman, "I guess we can't expect everything to do its duty." He stood up from planting the last of the cabbage slips. "Hold the basket over here," he said, starting down another row, "and I'll pick these tomatoes."

When he put an unusually big one into the basket, Kate said, "They know there's a war being fought!"

"Yes," said her father, "tomatoes are very patriotic. But come on, let's get washed up and go meet your mother."

Mrs. Coleman had spent the afternoon in Atlanta and was returning home on the six o'clock bus. She and some of her friends went into Atlanta on Saturdays; it had been a custom for as far back as Kate could remember. In earlier years, they had shopped or gone to a movie; it was their afternoon away from home. After the war started, they had continued to go to Atlanta, but they spent their time doing volunteer work. Some of them served coffee and doughnuts in the canteen at Terminal Station; some rolled bandages for the Red Cross; and others worked at military hospitals. Mrs. Coleman, who was a talented pianist, went to Lawson General Hospital to entertain wounded veterans.

Mr. Coleman and Kate walked to the drugstore that also served as Redhill's bus station. It was only three blocks from where they lived. The bus arrived at the same time they did, and Mrs. Coleman greeted her family. After chatting for a few moments with friends who had gotten off the bus, they started home. On the way, Kate asked her mother, "Did you play the piano today?"

"No, someone else had volunteered, so I did other things."

"What other things?"

"I wrote letters for men who can't write."

"You mean they don't know how?"

"They know how," said Mrs. Coleman, and Mr. Coleman added, "A man has to be literate before the military will have him. Maybe that'll keep me out!" Kate laughed.

Just then she saw Alice King and her little brother on the sidewalk across the street, and she crossed over to talk to them. She did not catch up with her parents again until they were home.

Mrs. Coleman made waffles for supper, a favorite with all three Colemans. During the meal Kate said suddenly, "I know why the men needed someone to write letters for them. Their arms had been broken and were in casts."

"Bright girl!" said Mr. Coleman. "Now pass the syrup."

"Some of the men had their arms in casts," said Mrs. Coleman. "Others had no arms to be in casts." Kate was silent, and her mother continued, "Others had bandages over their eyes and couldn't see to write."

"Will they be able to see when the bandages are off?" asked Kate.

"Some will; some won't," replied Mrs. Coleman. "I wrote a letter for one man who won't regain his sight, but he hasn't told his family yet. He has a wife in Tacoma, Washington, and she knows that he'll be home soon, but she doesn't know that his injury has left him blind. His former employer had asked her to find out if he wanted his old job back."

"Does he?" asked Mr. Coleman.

"He was a commercial artist," said Mrs. Coleman. "He had me write his wife, saying she should tell the boss that he was tired of that kind of work and wanted to look around for something else. When I read his letter back to him, he had me change 'look around' to 'hunt around' and laughed as if he had made a marvelous joke."

Mr. Coleman said, "Maybe next week you can go back to playing the piano."

"I'll work wherever I'm needed," she answered. Then she smiled. "And the letters weren't all sad. Several of them were funny, and one was mean."

"What was it about?" asked Kate.

"It was to a man's wife, warning her not to dare let her brothers or her father wear his overcoat while he was away!"

Kate and her parents laughed. "It's a real tragedy," said Mr. Coleman, "when a man can't feel safe about the overcoat he left behind. Like Robert E. Lee said, 'War is hell!' "

"Robert E. Lee said nothing of the sort," said Mrs. Coleman. "He knew it, but he didn't say it. General Sherman said it!"

"Just wanted to see how much history you knew!" said Mr. Coleman, winking at Kate. Then he said, "I know what let's do. Let's invite the Shaws over." The Shaws were Dudley and his parents.

"Let's do," said Kate. "Let's invite them and their checkerboard!"

Chinese checkers and other games were popular in Redhill.

Since the war and gas and tire rationing had cut down on travel, people turned to a variety of stay-at-home activities. The Colemans had a Monopoly board, and often they and the Shaws kept a game of it going for a long time. Then they would switch off to Chinese checkers or a card game that all six of them could play. Another of their pastimes was putting together jigsaw puzzles so difficult that assembling them might take everybody's spare time for a week.

"The Shaws are not at home," said Mrs. Coleman. "Liz told me this morning that they were to eat supper tonight with her folks."

"Well, I'll think of something else," said Mr. Coleman.

"I'll think of washing dishes," said Mrs. Coleman, starting to clear the table. Looking at the clock on the mantelpiece, she added, "It's time for the 'Hit Parade' if anybody wants to run turn on the radio."

Kate went into the sitting room and turned on the big cabinet radio. By the time it had warmed up, "The Hit Parade" was already underway. The number eight song of the week, "Coming in on a Wing and a Prayer," was being played. Mr. Coleman and Kate started singing it, and when Mrs. Coleman said that she had just as soon hear the featured vocalist, they sang even louder and more off-key.

"Thank goodness, it's over!" said Mrs. Coleman when it ended. "And in spite of all the noise, I've just had a brainstorm. Let's go on a picnic tomorrow. I'll devil some eggs and make sandwiches. How about it?"

"Great!" said Mr. Coleman. "We'll have it in the backyard."

Mrs. Coleman asked, "Don't you think maybe there's enough gas to get us to Warm Springs or some place?"

"Not a chance," said Mr. Coleman; and Kate groaned. "I'm sorry," he continued, "but that's the way it is. There's barely enough gas for me to get back and forth to work next week, and we don't have a ration coupon for buying more till Friday. There's a war on, you know!"

"We know!" said Kate and her mother at the same time.

"Like Robert E. Lee said—" said Mrs. Coleman. "Oh, well, never mind!"

The
Hideout

MONDAY MORNING, after roll call, Miss Jordan said, "As soon as I've collected lunch money, we'll start getting ready to move."

Hope Nelson said, "Lunch money? I didn't know we'd keep using the lunchroom."

Miss Jordan laughed. "Why, Hope, where did you think we'd eat?"

"I brought my lunch," said Hope.

"Of course, we'll continue to use the lunchroom," explained Miss Jordan. "The walk to it will be a bit farther, but we're strong!" The entire school system shared a lunchroom. It was in back of the high school, not far from where Kate lived, and had once been a gymnasium. Classes from grammar school walked to it in good weather and were taken there by bus during rainy spells.

Dinah Myrtle Moore asked, "Will we still go around by the courthouse?"

"As far as I know," said Miss Jordan, "that's the only possible route."

Oscar Yates said, "Dinah Myrtle's worried about her boyfriend."

"*One* of my boyfriends," said Dinah Myrtle.

The boyfriend worked at the filling station across from the courthouse, and whenever the sixth grade went past, he would prop against a gas pump and grin at Dinah Myrtle. Kate thought they were both silly. If Dinah Myrtle had ever thought of anything besides boys, she would be in the ninth grade instead of the sixth.

"Now," said Miss Jordan, "let's be getting ready. All of you will carry your own books, and if some of you boys will help me, we'll take our wall calendar and maps and the things from my desk." Pointing at the fish bowl, she added, "And, of course, we'll take Guppy and Whale." Guppy was not a guppy, nor was Whale a whale. Both were ordinary goldfish. One was slightly bigger than the other; he was Whale.

Zack Poe took down the big maps as soon as Miss Jordan mentioned that someone should be in charge of moving them, and Melvin Attaway grabbed the calendar. Henry Inman got to the goldfish bowl first, but Tubby Elrod tried to take it away from him. Water sloshed onto the floor, and Miss Jordan said, "Tubby, suppose you take these," holding out a pair of bookends. Then she asked Henry, "Will more water spill if you try to carry it? Maybe you should pour some of it off."

Henry went over to the window and slowly began pouring water from the bowl. "Hey!" he yelled. "Guppy fell out!"

"Pick him up quickly!" directed Miss Jordan.

"He fell out the window," said Henry.

"Then someone run to the yard in a hurry!"

39

All the boys and Kate made a dash for the door, but Miss Jordan headed off all but Kate and Alex Bronson, who were out before she could stop one of them. A moment later Kate handed Guppy to Henry; then she and Alex started to climb in the window instead of coming back through the building. They saw Miss Dillman as she came into the room.

Miss Jordan, watching Dudley move a small table that had been knocked over in the race to the door, looked up. "Oh, excuse us if we're a bit noisy," she said. "We're moving into our new building."

"It sounds as if you're tearing down this one," said Miss Dillman. Then she saw Alex and Kate. "Look!" she screamed. "They're coming in the window!"

"Yes, I see," said Miss Jordan. "Aren't they clever?"

Miss Dillman turned and stalked back across the hall, almost bumping into Mr. Bronson, who was coming into the room. "Is everybody ready?" he asked cheerfully. "I'm going to see you to your new quarters."

The sixth graders gathered up their belongings. Some of them helped Miss Jordan with the books from her desk. Zack, who had his own books and the big roll of maps, insisted that he could also take the dictionary. "It's too heavy for you," he explained, taking it from her.

"We'll march two abreast," said Mr. Bronson, "and let's look snappy as we go along."

The students marched through the building two abreast and looked as snappy as they knew how. At the end of the hall the procession was stopped when Mr. Bronson discovered that Nathan Oliver had brought the erasers from the blackboard. "It's my week to keep them dusted," explained Nathan. "We take turns."

"Go put them back," ordered Mr. Bronson. "We've installed a makeshift blackboard in your new room, and erasers have been supplied."

The class waited until Nathan returned; then they set out across the schoolyard. They marched two abreast and tried to look snappy again, until Nola May remembered that she had left her handkerchief with a dime tied in a knot in one corner of it by the window. She had put it there when Guppy had fallen onto the school ground.

"Hurry and get it!" said Miss Jordan.

When Nola May was back, the boys and girls, led by Mr. Bronson and Miss Jordan, crossed the street. They walked along the wide driveway that was shared by the Patersons and the Rigbys.

Past the garages, one for each family, the driveway became a trail, with flower and vegetable gardens on each side. Next there were two small paddocks with a barn for each one. The Patersons kept a riding horse in theirs, and the Rigbys had a milk cow. Then came the huts.

Mr. Bronson stopped at the first one. "This is to be yours," he said. It was on the Paterson side of the trail. "The other one is for the seventh grade."

Almost everyone groaned, and Miss Jordan asked, "Did you say the seventh grade?"

"Yes, I did," said Mr. Bronson; and Kate thought to herself, Just when everything's going good, something spoils it!

Alex Bronson turned to his father. "But Miss Dillman teaches the seventh grade!"

"Why, yes, so she does. What's so strange about that?"

"We thought the fifth grade was coming."

"That was the original plan. But the Superintendent sent word this morning to have the seventh grade move instead. But come on, let's have a look inside." He led the way into the hut, the boys and girls grumbling among themselves over the news that Miss Dillman's grade was to be their only neighbor.

Inside, there were desks of various sizes that had been brought from classrooms that could spare them. A blackboard was at one end of the room, and there was a chair with a table, instead of a desk, for Miss Jordan.

"This isn't exactly a palace, is it?" said Mr. Bronson, smiling. "But after all, there's a war on!"

"It don't look any better than home," said Winnie Owens, as if she expected any place she went to school to be an improvement over where she lived. The Owens family lived in a ramshackle house in the country. All the sixth graders, whether they lived in big houses or small ones, looked as if they weren't sure they wanted to come to school here after all. Then Kate said, "Mr. Bronson, I like it!"

That was all that was needed to bring approval from her classmates. The boys began saying the place looked all right to them, and the girls agreed. Nola May said, "Why, it's just as beautiful as can be!"

Mr. Bronson laughed then and asked everyone to find a place to sit. There were not enough desks for everybody to have a separate one, so Kate and Tootie sat together, and Zack and Dudley shared a desk.

Mr. Bronson talked about the new location. "There'll be some things you'll like and some you won't," he said. "For instance, the ones of you who ride the buses will have to walk back up to the main building to catch them." The students who rode buses looked as if the bit of extra walking would kill them. Mr. Bronson added, "But I doubt you'll mind getting out of school ten minutes early in order to be there on time." That put everyone in a good humor again.

Mr. Bronson pointed out the window. "I'm sure you know what the little building down the path is, don't you?"

"A privy," answered Melvin Attaway. "We've got one just like it at home."

"It's an outhouse," said Winnie Owens.

"Well, anyway," continued Mr. Bronson, "that will be the girls' rest room, and the one in back of the seventh grade we'll designate as the boys' rest room. It's not as convenient as we might wish, but then we haven't always had running water."

"Where I live, we don't have it yet," said Winnie. She did not sound as if she were complaining, only that she was making it clear that an outhouse was nothing new to her.

"Us neither," said Zack and Tootie, who were echoed by still others. Almost everyone who lived in town had running water by now, but not everyone who lived in the country did. Electricity had only been available in rural Georgia in recent years. When power lines had been installed, most families had had their homes wired, replacing kerosene lamps with electric lights, but not all of them had been able to afford water pumping systems at the same time.

"The Patersons have a spigot at the end of their garden," said Mr. Bronson, "and they've consented for us to use it for our fresh water. We've put a bucket and dipper in each hut, and you boys will want to haul water whenever it's needed. There'll be wash pans and soap, and there are paper cups for today, but each one of you should bring a glass or cup from home for use after this. And that's not as convenient as having drinking fountains, but again, it's a system that was used in earlier times, except that water was drawn then in buckets from a well."

"We still get ours that way," said Winnie, and a chorus of "Us too," went up around the room.

Mr. Bronson continued. "I'm sorry that the whole grammar school can't be under one roof, but as long as we're having to take this temporary measure, I must commend you on being willing to make the most of it." He looked around. "It's rustic, but in the old days a lot of people went to school in just such buildings as this. One-room schoolhouses, they were called. Only in them, instead of a single grade, there were many."

None of the children looked especially interested, but Mr. Bronson went on. "However, I admit this one looks more primitive than some of the one-room schoolhouses I've seen." Chuckling, he added, "It looks more like an outpost, or even a gangster's hideout. In fact, you might pretend it's a hideout instead of a schoolhouse."

"Good idea!" said his son, Alex. "It's a hideout, and we're all outlaws."

Zack hopped up. "And I'm the leader," he announced. "Alex, you guard the front door, and Dudley, you guard the back."

"Now settle down, students!" said Mr. Bronson.

"But we're not students!" said Alex.

"That's right!" said Zack. "We're outlaws, and we've captured our first prisoner."

Mr. Bronson smiled. "Who?" he asked.

"You!" said Zack. "Quick, somebody, find a rope!"

Lawmaking

"Now just sit down!" said Mr.
Bronson so loudly that even Alex sat down. The students were
quiet, and Mr. Bronson, sounding pleasant again, said, "I take it
all back. Kindly do not regard this hut as a hideout or yourselves
as outlaws. We must think of something better."

Miss Jordan said, "With two houses down here, could we
maybe pretend that one is the Senate and the other is the House of
Representatives?"

"Indeed we could!" said Mr. Bronson. He added, "And I'll be
President!" as proudly as Zack had claimed to be the leader of the
outlaws. "Then all of you can aid me in doing my job. Since
you're not in the same building with me, I'll need your help,
won't I?"

They agreed that yes, he would need their help. "Why don't
you be the House of Representatives," he suggested, "and let the
seventh grade be the Senate? You can introduce bills, and if
they're passed in both houses, they can be sent to me. Then, if I

sign them, they'll become laws." He looked out the window toward the grammar-school building. "I'll stay busy most of the time in my office on Capitol Hill!" He chuckled over his joke.

Kate raised her hand. "What kind of bills could we pass?"

"Well, almost anything having to do with running the classrooms down here. With the war on and the labor shortage what it is, we'll only have Mr. Ard to do all our janitorial work, and, of course, keeping the main building clean is a full-time job. So maybe you'll introduce legislation to help him. You could vote to have someone from each grade take trash cans to the incinerator every day, and you could decide about washing blackboards and that sort of thing."

Nathan Oliver said, "But this week I'm supposed to dust the erasers. Won't it still be my turn?"

Mr. Bronson smiled. "You may have to discuss it with your fellow congressmen. On anything that concerns the sixth grade only, you won't need to bring in the Senate. I see no reason that a House of Representatives couldn't govern itself in some matters."

The students did not look pleased to learn that the matters he had in mind had to do with work and keeping things clean, but they cheered up when he said, "And at the same time you might help Miss Jordan decide such things as when your recess period should be. Since you're separate from any other building, you won't have to arrange your schedule to suit anyone else's—as long as you don't make so much noise that you interfere with the seventh grade. How does that sound?"

"Fine!" chorused the class.

"I must leave now and get back to Capitol Hill!" Mr. Bronson thought that was funnier than the class did. "I'll bring the Senate to its chambers across the avenue in a few minutes. Meanwhile you can get organized. Elect yourselves a Speaker of the House, and you'll be in business. All right, Miss Jordan, they're all yours."

"Oh, thank you, Mr. President!" said Miss Jordan, and everybody laughed.

As soon as Mr. Bronson had gone, Henry Inman and Glenn Rigby, who knew where the Patersons' garden spigot was located, went for a bucketful of water. When they returned, everyone had a drink of it. "Write your names on the cups so that you can use them again," said Miss Jordan. "And now let's get out our English books. Today we'll continue with adjectives."

Nathan Oliver said, "But Mr. Bronson wanted us to elect a Speaker."

"So he did!" said Miss Jordan. "Do I hear any nominations for the job?"

"I nominate me," said Louise Lockwood.

"Aw, you can't nominate yourself!" said Oscar Yates.

"I can so. Can't I, Miss Jordan?"

"Well, I think it might be better if someone else did."

"Then I nominate Hope Nelson to nominate me," said Louise.

"O.K.," said Hope cheerily. "I nominate Louise Lockwood."

Oscar said, "And I nominate Dudley. I think a boy ought to be Speaker of the House."

"I think a man ought to!" said Zack Poe, standing up and beating himself on the chest. "I'm man enough to do the job if anybody would care to nominate me!"

"Nobody would care to nominate you," said Tootie. "But I nominate Kate Coleman."

Dinah Myrtle said, "Miss Jordan, I think a man—I mean, a boy—ought to be Speaker of the House."

"You would think that!" said Kate. Then she added, "I don't think it ought to have to be a boy, but I vote for Dudley anyway."

Tootie said, "But, Kate, I just nominated you!"

"You could take it back," suggested Kate.

"O.K.," said Tootie, "I take it back, and I'll vote for Dudley too."

"All in favor of Dudley, raise your hands," said Miss Jordan, and almost everyone in the class voted for him, including Hope Nelson. She said she hadn't realized when she nominated Louise that she would be expected to vote for her too. Those voting for Louise were Dudley, Louise herself, and Nola May, who voted for both candidates.

"Dudley, you're elected," said Miss Jordan. "Come up and preside."

Dudley went to the front of the room. "Anybody got laws or anything you want passed?"

Hands went up, and he recognized Kate. "I think recess ought to last longer than it does," she said.

Ivy said, "Say, that's a good idea!" and Dudley asked, "How about twice as long?"

"O.K.," said Kate. "But since this is our first day, I think it should start now and last till we want to come back inside."

"Everybody in favor raise your hand," said Dudley, and all the boys and girls raised their hands. At the same time they looked toward the back of the room, where Miss Jordan was sitting, to see if she was going to object. But her hand was up too.

"I don't think this kind of law is exactly what Mr. Bronson had in mind, but it's such a pretty day, and as Kate said, this is our first day here. So why don't we representatives adjourn for a while?" Holding up the English book, she said, "Use some adjectives while you're playing, and let's talk about them when we reconvene."

"Look!" said Dudley, pointing out the window. "Here come

the senators!" Mr. Bronson and Miss Dillman, followed by the entire seventh grade, were starting down the trail.

"Let's make spitballs and throw them at them!" said Tubby Elrod.

"Why, that's no way to welcome them!" said Miss Jordan. "I'm ashamed of you, Tubby!" She smiled as if she weren't really ashamed of him.

"I have an idea," said Alice King. "Let's stand outside and sing 'The Welcome Song' to them while they're going past."

"That's a splendid idea," said Miss Jordan. "Quickly, everybody, outside!"

The class piled out of its hut and stood in front till the seventh grade got almost to them, then they began singing "The Welcome Song." The words were:

> Hello, Everybody, and how do you do?
> We are here to shout it out: WELCOME ALL OF YOU!
> Hello, Friends and Neighbors, come join in the fun,
> And we'll sing it louder still: WELCOME EVERYONE!

Mr. Bronson smiled, but Miss Dillman did not. The students waved and grinned, and some of the seventh-grade boys stepped out of line and took playful pokes at their sixth-grade buddies. When Miss Dillman looked back and saw them, she yelled, "Get back in line. School is not a picnic! Did you hear me? School is not a picnic!" She said it so loudly that people on the far side of Redhill could have heard her.

"The Welcome Song" was sung two more times, and by then the seventh grade was inside its hut.

"Now, that was a proper welcome!" said Miss Jordan. "You deserve your long recess. Just don't go too near the Senate, and try to keep down the noise."

"That's right, you guys," said Zack, shaking his fist at his class-mates. "School is not a picnic!"

Everyone laughed, including Miss Jordan. "Oh, I don't know, Zack," she said. "There's no reason it shouldn't be!"

Target
Practice

At first the sixth and seventh grades called their new location "Congress," but everyone else called it "Hut School." Soon it was called Hut School by everybody, even by the members of Congress.

During the first week it was in session, the House of Representatives introduced a number of bills. Kate told her father about them on Sunday afternoon when the two of them were out walking. They had gone into the woods back of the Jefferson place. The Jeffersons were an elderly couple who lived across the street from the Colemans.

"Does Mr. Bronson ever veto any of your bills?" asked Mr. Coleman.

"He hasn't yet," said Kate, "but the only ones that get sent to him are about ways for us to help Mr. Ard keep things clean. Anything else gets killed off by Miss Dillman. She threw the last bill into the trash can without even showing it to the senators."

"That wasn't very democratic of her," said Mr. Coleman. "What was it about?"

"We voted to have the seventh grade sweep out both huts every afternoon." When Mr. Coleman laughed, Kate hurried on. "Well, that would help Mr. Ard! And they've got a broom, and we haven't." Then she laughed with her father. "Miss Jordan thought maybe we should put through a bill to have everybody share the broom, but we liked our way better, so she let us try it."

"No use doing your own work if you can persuade somebody else to do it for you!" said Mr. Coleman.

"Look!" said Kate, pointing ahead. "There's Hut School!" One end of the seventh-grade hut could be seen through the woods.

"Yes, of course," said her father. "It's been there all the time!"

"I knew it was in this direction," said Kate, "but I didn't know it was so near." Usually in their walks she and her father took a different route through the woods, coming out at a stream in back of the high school.

"Distances and directions can fool you when there are mostly trees around," said Mr. Coleman.

Kate motioned in the direction she and her father usually walked. "The lunchroom is right through there," she said. "And if Hut School is here, why, we could go through these woods every day to get to lunch, couldn't we?"

"It would be a shortcut all right," agreed her father. "Come on, let's walk it now!" He led the way out of the woods and across a barbed-wire fence into the small pasture that belonged to the Olsons. They lived next door to the Colemans, on the opposite side from the Shaws, but their pasture was across the street.

Just as they started through the pasture, a big calf came out from behind a clump of bushes and started toward Kate.

"A friend of yours?" asked her father.

"This is Ferdinand," said Kate. "He's let Dudley and me pet

him since he was a day old. The Olsons kept him in that little pen near their barn till recently."

The calf put his head down and pawed at the earth with one foot. "He's trying to act grown-up," said Kate. "But he still likes to play. Watch this!" She ran across the pasture, and Ferdinand chased after her. They circled back to where they began.

Mr. Coleman patted the young bull on the head. Then he and Kate started walking again. Ferdinand followed them, stopping every now and then to put his head down and paw the earth as if he were about to attack. Mr. Coleman said to him, "You're not supposed to want to fight, not with a name like Ferdinand!"

"Mr. Olson let Dudley and me decide what to call him," said Kate. "But if he's not going to be gentle like Ferdinand in the story, we may have to think of something else."

Soon she and her father crossed a fence into the weed patch at the back of the high school property. Ferdinand, on the opposite side of the barbed wire, put his head down and gave a weak bellow as they left. "Keep trying, pal!" called Mr. Coleman. Then he told Kate, "You see how near the lunchroom we are. I'd think the authorities would let you use the shortcut."

He started toward the road but turned when Kate asked, "Why don't we check on the stream now that we're this near?"

They walked across the weed patch, where goldenrod was in full bloom, and into the woods. Soon they arrived at the stream, and Kate looked for a narrow place where she could jump across it. Suddenly there was a rifle shot. "Hey!" yelled Mr. Coleman. "Careful where you aim!"

A man laughed. "We wouldn't shoot you, not even for a reward!" Then he came through the trees. It was Mr. Shaw, followed by Dudley. "Didn't mean to scare you," he said. "And actually, we're being careful where we aim. Dudley and I found a box of bullets we didn't know we had, so we decided to come down here. We've found us a good bank through there that's just right for target practice. Come on and try your luck."

"Let's do!" said Kate. She was afraid that if she didn't speak up quickly her father would say they'd better not. There was a time when she had gone occasionally with Dudley and his father to the Flint River swamp for target practice with guns that Mr. Shaw collected. But that was before gas was rationed and when there was no shortage of bullets either. Mr. Coleman had never gone with them; he was not especially interested in guns.

At the bank the target was a big piece of cardboard. Circles were drawn on it, one inside another, with a big dot in the center. "Ladies first!" said Mr. Shaw, handing Kate the rifle. "Let's see you hit the bull's-eye!"

Kate took the rifle, unlatched the safety guard, and took careful aim. She was glad the 22-caliber rifle was being used; she had fired it lots of times when they used to go to the swamp.

"You missed!" said Dudley.

"She hit the middle ring," said Mr. Shaw, after the target had been examined.

Dudley fired next, and his bullet went in the outer ring. So did Mr. Shaw's. "Kate's in the lead," said Mr. Shaw, handing the rifle to Mr. Coleman.

"What do I do now?" asked Mr. Coleman.

"You shoot!" said Mr. Shaw.

"Just point the gun and pull the trigger, I guess," said Mr. Coleman, taking awkward aim.

"You really don't know anything about guns, do you?" said Mr. Shaw.

"I somehow never learned about such things. I don't know that I even want to learn!"

"Sure you do!" said Mr. Shaw. "Here, let me show you." He tapped the sights and told Mr. Coleman how to line them up. "When you think you're on the target, fire away!"

Mr. Coleman took aim again; then he said, "Nothing happens when I pull the trigger."

Kate and Dudley laughed. "You have to let go the safety," said Dudley; and Kate showed her father how to do it. He took aim again and fired, missing the entire piece of cardboard.

"Maggie's drawers!" said Kate and Dudley at the same time. They had heard that in military target practice if anyone missed the target altogether, a red flag was waved in the air and that it was called Maggie's drawers.

"You get another try," said Mr. Shaw. "We all do." He handed the rifle to Kate, and the target practice continued. When the bullets were used up, Kate had hit the bull's-eye once and the middle circle three times. Dudley had hit the middle one every time, but he had not scored a bull's-eye at all. Mr. Shaw's aim had proved best, but Mr. Coleman's was so poor that he had hit the cardboard only once. It was with the last bullet, and Mr. Shaw teased him. "Dazzling!" he said, and everybody laughed as they started home together.

After supper, when Kate told her mother about discovering the shortcut to the lunchroom, Mrs. Coleman said, "I'm glad you're more interested in school than you were at first."

"Oh, yes," said Kate. "School is fun!"

"You must be mistaken," said her father, pretending to be serious. "School is *never* fun."

"Yes, it is," insisted Kate. "I like everything about Hut School except Miss Dillman. We could have had a good time Friday if it hadn't been for her."

"She's probably a very capable teacher," said Mrs. Coleman.

"She's mean," said Kate. "The sixth grade challenged the seventh grade to a game of softball in the afternoon, but Miss Dillman said, 'Indeed not!' and made her class stay inside because they hadn't all made a hundred in spelling."

"She does sound a bit stern," said Mr. Coleman. "But aren't there enough of you in the sixth grade to have a ball game by yourselves?"

"Yes, but the only open space is between the two huts. So when the seventh grade doesn't join us, we have to stay on the other side of our room and be quiet or she'll complain to Mr. Bronson. I hate ol' hatchet-faced Dillman."

"Now, Kate, that's disrespectful," said her mother.

"Yes, it is," agreed Mr. Coleman. "Everybody is not alike, and Miss Dillman can't help it if she has a more sober nature than some of us. You should refer to her as *somber but solid, firm but fair, priggish but prudent hatchet-faced Dillman*."

He and Kate laughed, but Mrs. Coleman did not. "You mustn't hate anyone," she said.

"We hate the Germans and the Japanese, don't we?" said Kate. "We're trying to kill them."

"We're defending ourselves," said her mother. "They started the killing, and who knows when it will all end. But maybe someday wars will cease, and no one will hate—or kill—anyone else."

Kate changed the subject back to Hut School. "We've decided that from now on the House of Representatives will quit trying to work out anything with the Senate. Mr. Bronson told us that on matters that concerned just us we could make our own decisions. We may vote in a holiday for ourselves one day next week!"

"Oh, my goodness!" said her mother. "You'll try to put a stop to that, won't you?"

"Put a stop to it?" said Kate. "I'm the one who thought it up!" Again she and her father laughed.

Mrs. Coleman said, "Perhaps I should tell you: there's talk about Miss Jordan. Some people think she's not a good teacher."

"Why, she is so!" said Kate.

"You used to say she treated sixth graders like babies."

"Well, after we got her over that, she's been great."

Mr. Coleman said, "I don't know why anyone would criticize her. The students are making real progress in their studies; I can tell they are from the work Kate and Dudley have accomplished already, and what's more, they seem to be enjoying learning."

"I'm afraid that's why Miss Jordan is suspect," said Mrs. Coleman. "You and I know that it's possible to learn and be happy at the same time, but many people feel that school should be as unpleasant as a dose of castor oil. Anyway, Kate, I hope you'll withdraw your bill for a holiday for the sixth grade only."

Mr. Coleman said, "I don't think Miss Jordan would let anyone go quite that far."

"She might!" said Kate happily.

"Yes, she might," agreed her mother. "But she would be the one to get in trouble with parents and the School Board. How fair would that be to her?"

Kate did not answer, but she knew her mother was right. "I'll go turn on the radio," she said. "It's time for Charlie McCarthy."

Mr. Coleman looked at his watch and then at the clock on the mantelpiece. "The clock has stopped," he said. "I'm afraid we've missed Charlie. But turn the radio on anyway. It's time for 'One Man's Family.' "

58

Kate turned on the radio and waited for it to warm up, but it made a loud, sputtering noise instead. "There's too much static," she said, switching off the knob.

"In that case," said Mr. Coleman, "let's see if your mother won't play the piano for us."

"Let's do!" said Kate.

Mrs. Coleman got up and started toward the piano. "See," said Mr. Coleman, winking at Kate, "she's more reliable than a radio!"

Letters to
Soldiers

DINAH MYRTLE MOORE said she didn't want to walk through the woods and across a pasture, even a little one, to get to the lunchroom. She would rather go around by the courthouse square—and the filling station where her boyfriend worked. But everyone else was in favor of using the shortcut, and the bill passed in the House of Representatives by 23 to 1. Kate was surprised that Miss Dillman and the seventh graders favored the legislation too, and when the bill was presented to Mr. Bronson, he was as enthusiastic about it as if it had been his idea. He said that he would discuss the matter with the Superintendent immediately.

When he left, Miss Jordan said, "Isn't it nice to have come up with a bill that pleases everybody?"

"Everybody but me," said Dinah Myrtle.

"That's right," agreed Miss Jordan. "But you'll like the shortcut, I'm sure. And I'm just sorry Tootie and Zack have missed out on the fun today. Finally we get a bill through the Senate and signed by the President, and they're not here to enjoy it with us. Do any of you know if they're sick?"

"No, ma'am," said Melvin Attaway, who was a neighbor of the Poes. "Ain't nothing wrong. It's just *that time of year;* that's all." He got up from his desk and went over to the fish bowl. It was his day to feed Guppy and Whale.

"What do you mean, 'that time of year?'"

"Time to pick cotton," said Melvin, sprinkling a small amount of fish food on to the water.

Kate knew that the Poes dropped out of school every year when cotton was ready to be picked. She explained to Miss Jordan, "They'll come back eventually."

"But they shouldn't drop out at all," said Miss Jordan. "School has been in session only two weeks."

"Yes," said Kate, "but it's time for cotton to be picked anyway, and Mr. Poe always makes his family stay home and help with the work."

Winnie Owens said, "I have to help my folks pick cotton too."

"Me too," said more than half the sixth graders. Almost everyone who lived in the country lived on a farm, and cotton was the main crop.

"But you won't drop out of school to do it, will you?" asked Miss Jordan.

"No, ma'am," said Winnie. "The rest of us pick after school and on Saturdays."

Ivy Holbrook said, "In some places in south Georgia, schools close so cotton can be picked."

"Say," said Henry, "that would be great!"

Ivy added, "But they have to start school in midsummer to make up for it."

"That wouldn't be so great, would it, Henry?" said Miss Jordan. "But tell me, when will Tootie and Zack return to school?"

Dudley said, "By Thanksgiving."

"Thanksgiving!" said Miss Jordon as if she couldn't believe it.

"One time it was nearly Christmas before they got back."

"But isn't there a law against keeping anyone out of school?"

"It's seasonal labor," said Alex. "I've heard my father talk about it. The law can't make anybody stay in school if that's the reason for staying out."

"Well, it's a shame," said Miss Jordan. Kate had never seen her look so upset. "It does seem as if Mr. Poe could hire someone to help with the work instead of keeping his children out of school."

"Mr. Poe never does hire anybody to help with work that his family can do," said Melvin. "But with the war on and everything he couldn't find anybody even if he wanted to. Nearly all the men are off in the Army."

"Some are in the Navy," said Glenn; and Henry Inman added, "And the Marines."

Melvin said, "And some of the ones still at home are working in places that make guns and things."

Nola May said, "The man who used to help my daddy do his farmwork has a job now at the bomber plant." She was talking about Bell Aircraft Company, in Marietta, where planes were made. It was called Bell Bomber, or the bomber plant, in the part of Georgia where it was located.

"I know that a lot of people have gone to work in war industries," said Miss Jordan, "and that a lot of others are in service, but I didn't know that it had become necessary for the farm load to be carried by little children."

Kate said, "Miss Jordan, we're not little children." She wished that she hadn't said it; Miss Jordan looked so sad about Zack and

Tootie that she wished she had said something to cheer her up instead. But Miss Jordan smiled at her and said softly, "We're all little children." Then she said, "Maybe now we'd better get back to lessons. Let's see. What did we do in English yesterday?"

"We talked about letter writing," answered Kate.

"Yes, now I remember, and today how would each one of you like to write a personal letter to someone?"

Sylvia said, "I'd like to write to my grandmother."

"I'd like to write one of my boyfriends," said Dinah Myrtle, and her classmates snickered.

"We didn't have a lesson in writing love letters, did we, Miss Jordan?" asked Tubby Elrod, and everybody laughed.

Ivy Holbrook said, "I'm going to write to my brother. He's in—"

Oscar interrupted her. "We know, he's in the Army overseas. Just like a lot of other people! And before that, he went to school wherever it was you lived before you came here, and he was a big shot."

"He was a football player," said Ivy. Then to Miss Jordan, she said, "I think it would be nice if everybody wrote a letter to our men in uniform."

"'Our men in uniform,'" said Oscar, imitating Ivy. "She's trying to act like a grown-up. They're always talking about 'our men in uniform.'"

"Now, Oscar," said Miss Jordan, "we're grateful to everybody who's fighting so that the rest of us can be free."

"Well, some have to stay home so the rest of us can be free," said Oscar. "And Ivy acts like her brother is the only person who's doing anything to help."

"I'm sure Ivy doesn't feel that way," said Miss Jordan. "Melvin's brother is in the Army too, and Louise's is in the Navy, and others of you have relatives or friends in the war. Maybe we really should write to them today. If any of you don't have some-one special who's in service, why not write to the ones we've mentioned?"

The letter writing began, and in a few moments Henry Inman said, "I'm finished."

"So soon?" asked Miss Jordan.

"Yes, ma'am. I wrote Louise's brother, Wade." Holding up his letter he said, "Here's what I wrote: 'Dear Wade. Don't get killed or anything. Your friend, Henry Inman.'"

The students laughed, but Miss Jordan did not. "I think it might be nicer to write something else. Why not try another letter? You live near Louise, don't you?"

"Yes, ma'am."

"Then you must know her brother quite well. Tell him about something that's happened since he's been away."

"His girl friend is going out with somebody else," said Henry. "That's happened."

Louise snapped, "They broke up before he left!"

"They broke up lots of times before he left," said Henry, "but they always went back together. But he's too far off now for them to make up!"

"He may not want to make up," said Louise.

"Wouldn't do any good if he did!" said Henry.

"Here now, no arguments!" said Miss Jordan. "Henry, I'm certain that you'll be able to think of something that will be just right for your letter."

The students went back to work, and when it was almost time for school to be out, Miss Jordan suggested that they stop.

Sylvia Gage asked, "Do you want us to hand in our letters?"

"No," said Miss Jordan.

"Aren't you going to correct them?" asked Sylvia. "I worked hard on mine."

"I'm glad that you did," said Miss Jordan, "but no, I'm not going to correct them. Tomorrow we might invent characters and write to them, and maybe then I'll read the letters to see if I can be of help to you. But with the ones today, let's let them be between you and whomever you've written. After all, personal letters are personal." Then she said, "But, Henry, I hope you wrote your letter without bringing up the subject of death or anyone's ex-girl friend."

"Yes, ma'am, I told Wade about our hogs instead. Ellie Bell, our ol' brood sow, had fourteen pigs on Sunday morning."

"Really?" said Miss Jordan. "Fourteen?"

"Yes, ma'am, but she ate three of them."

"Oh, my!" said Miss Jordan.

"But she hasn't bothered the rest, so I wrote Wade about them. Do you think that's O.K.?"

"I think that's fine," said Miss Jordan. "He'll be happy to hear from you, I'm sure, and with his farm background he may not be upset that Ellie Bell ate three of her children! But I confess that it shocks me to the core!" She laughed with her students then.

"Will you mail my letter?" asked Henry.

"I'll be glad to," said Miss Jordan. "Louise, if you'll bring me the address tomorrow, I'll mail the letters to Wade." Other boys and girls began handing her letters.

"We wrote Melvin's brother," said Alice King, speaking for herself and Hope Nelson.

"So did I," said Glenn Rigby and Tubby Elrod at the same time. Melvin said, "Mamma'll be writing him tonight or tomorrow, and she'll send ours along." The students who had written to his brother handed him their letters.

Ivy asked, "What about my brother, Miss Jordan? I know his address by heart. Will you mail his letters?"

"Certainly," said Miss Jordan, taking Ivy's letter. "Who else has a letter for Ivy's brother?"

Ivy looked around to see which of her classmates had written to her brother, but no hands went up. Then Kate raised her hand. "I haven't quite finished," she said, which was not an outright lie. "I was trying to think of something else to say. Could I finish the letter at home and bring it tomorrow?"

"Surely you could," said Miss Jordan, who looked pleased that someone else had written to Ivy's brother.

Kate had not been writing to him. She had started a letter to a cousin of her mother's who was in a training camp up North. But somehow it hadn't seemed right that no one except Ivy had written to Marcus Holbrook, even if Ivy did bore everybody by talking about him all the time. Kate didn't know how she herself might feel if she had a brother and if he were in service. Maybe she would be so proud of him that she would act just like Ivy. And anyway Marcus couldn't help it that Ivy talked about him so much.

At home, after she'd had a glass of milk and a bread and jelly sandwich, she began the letter. At first it was not easy to think of anything to write. She did not know Marcus Holbrook well because he was already in the Army when his family moved to Redhill, but she had seen him a few times when he had been at home on furlough.

She wrote one paragraph about Hut School, and she thought of writing next about the convoy that went through town on Satur-

66

day. She and Dudley had seen the jeep at the head of it and had raced to the corner to watch the procession of military vehicles. No one watching it had known where the convoy was from or where it was headed. Some guessed it was from Fort Benning down in Columbus, heading to Fort McPherson in Atlanta, while others said it might have come from a fort or camp in Florida and could be on its way to almost anywhere. Kate decided that maybe she should not tell about it in her letter. She had heard a radio program once about keeping troop movements secret, and she would hate for her letter to fall into the hands of a spy somewhere. So instead she told Marcus that in case he was too far away to hear any music from the United States maybe he would like to know what songs were popular now. She told him that the most recent one to climb to the top of "Your Hit Parade" was "Sunday, Monday or Always." Then she listed other favorites, saying that if he would like to know the words to them, she would be glad to send them to him. She also told him about "Pistol-Packin' Mama," which was not among the "Hit Parade" choices yet, but she and her father believed it would become a winner. "And if you like slow songs," she wrote, "my mother is partial to one called 'People Will Say We're in Love.' "

She finished the letter just as Mrs. Coleman asked her to come and hold a skein of wool yarn while she wound it into a ball. She was going to knit a brown scarf for her cousin who was in the Army. While they worked with the yarn, Kate told her mother that she had written a letter to the cousin and one to Ivy's brother. "You know," she said, "I barely know Marcus Holbrook, but by the time I finished writing to him I felt almost as if we were good friends."

"There's something about letter writing that can give you that

67

feeling," agreed her mother. "And when Marcus gets your letter, I'm sure he'll feel as if he has heard from a friend."

Kate looked at the world globe her father kept on the table by his reading lamp. The family looked places up on it whenever new names and battles were reported in the news. "Marcus is probably halfway round the world," she said, giving the globe a spin. "It gives you a funny feeling, doesn't it, to write to somebody who's so far away?"

"Yes, it does," agreed her mother.

Kate went on, "And to think about how the letter will get there."

"Well," said Mrs. Coleman, "it will leave Redhill in a mailbag on the train, but eventually it will be put on a plane or a ship to cross the ocean."

Kate folded her letter and put it by the globe that was slowing to a halt. "And the ship might get torpedoed and sunk," she said, "or the plane might get shot down."

She expected her mother to say, "Oh, Kate, don't talk like that!" But Mrs. Coleman said, "Yes, that's true."

The Wartime
Home-Front Hero

THE SHORTCUT from Hut School
to the lunchroom was approved. The Jeffersons did not mind that
it led through their woods, and the Olsons were glad for the students to cross their pasture. The only stock in it besides Ferdinand
was a milk cow, and she stayed near the barn, where her new calf
was kept. The School Superintendent said the plan suited him
fine, and the next morning a high school shop class built wooden
stiles for the fences. Kate hadn't thought it would be any real
bother to climb between strands of barbed wire to get in and out
of the pasture, but she realized that the steps were more convenient.

On the first day the shortcut was used, Ferdinand hid in a
clump of bushes and did not come out. Kate supposed he was
puzzled that so many people were suddenly passing through his
territory. Or maybe he was frightened by all the noise Miss Dillman made. She and her students were ahead of the sixth grade,
and she yelled things like "Stay in line!" and "Don't dawdle!"

Ferdinand stayed in the bushes again the second day till Kate, near the end of the line, called to him. Then he came out and let her pat him. On the third day he ran along beside her, frisking about and pretending to be rambunctious. The sixth graders laughed at him, but the seventh graders did not see him. They were just ahead, as usual, and Miss Dillman was screaming at them to move along and stop laughing and talking. Miss Jordan didn't care how much her students laughed and talked on their way to lunch.

The next day Ferdinand came out from behind his screen of bushes when the seventh graders arrived at the pasture. He stood off to one side and looked at them. Miss Dillman, aggravated that some of the boys crossed the stile two steps at a time instead of going over it in what she called "an orderly fashion," was busy screaming at them and did not see Ferdinand until she crossed into the pasture. "WHAT'S THIS?" she called so loudly that her students stopped and turned around, and Miss Jordan and the sixth graders, in back, stopped too.

Ferdinand moved toward Miss Dillman, who moved away from him. He stopped and pawed at the earth, and she screamed, "He's going to attack me!" As if she had given him the idea, he lowered his head and shook it as though he were going to butt her, and she turned and started running. Ferdinand chased her as if it were the best game he had ever played, while the sixth and seventh graders and Miss Jordan laughed as if it were the best show they had ever seen.

Miss Dillman did not slow down until she was across the fence on the opposite side of the pasture. No one was sure whether her feet had touched any of the steps in crossing the stile or if she had somehow leaped across it. In any event she got over the barbed wire quickly. Everyone ran to catch up with her.

Ferdinand stood at the fence, allowing anyone who held out

70

a hand to pat him. Miss Jordan told Miss Dillman, "I thought I was a city slicker, but I believe you know even less about farm animals than I do. This one is harmless."

"It's a ferocious bull!" said Miss Dillman.

"Why, no," insisted Miss Jordan, "he's a playful calf." She looked at Ferdinand and added, "Aren't you?"

Ferdinand lowed as if in agreement, and everyone except Miss Dillman laughed hysterically. Kate didn't know when she'd ever thought anything was funnier.

Miss Dillman, out of breath from racing across the pasture, regained her strength and marched the seventh graders to lunch. Afterward she made them return to Hut School the long way around, but the sixth grade used the shortcut and got back in time to play three innings of ball before time to go inside.

In midafternoon Kate, who had finished an arithmetic test ahead of everyone else, thought about the excitement at lunchtime. If only Tootie and Zack had been there to enjoy it! Except for that, it was perfect. Just then Mr. Bronson appeared in the doorway of the hut. "If this is a convenient time," he said to Miss Jordan, "would you bring your students over to the seventh grade and let me talk to everybody?"

Glenn Rigby, frowning over the test, answered for Miss Jordan, "Yes, sir, this would be a real convenient time." Kate used to feel the same way about arithmetic, but recently, with Miss Jordan's help, she had begun to understand and then enjoy it. She had even taken it off the list of things she and her father planned to abolish someday.

"I was giving a test," said Miss Jordan pleasantly, "but the ones who haven't finished by now may need a bit of help from me in the days ahead. We'll be pleased to join you."

A few minutes later when the sixth graders had crowded into

the hut next door, Mr. Bronson began. His first announcement was about the shortcut. Because of Miss Dillman's fear of Ferdinand, the seventh grade was to go back to using the long route to the lunchroom unless someone could think of a better solution.

Louise Lockwood suggested that Miss Dillman just not go to lunch.

"What?" screamed Miss Dillman.

"I mean, let somebody bring you back a plate," said Louise, but Miss Dillman snorted at the idea. Then Henry Inman suggested that the Olsons be asked to keep Ferdinand in a pen.

"No!" said Kate and Dudley at the same time. "He was there first," added Dudley, while Kate asked Henry, "How would you like to be kept in a pen?"

Mr. Bronson said, "The Olsons were nice enough to let us use their pasture; I don't think we'd want them to deprive their livestock the use of it."

Miss Jordan suggested that since Kate and Dudley were friends and neighbors of the calf, they could pat him while everyone else crossed his pasture. That did not satisfy Miss Dillman either, and Mr. Bronson said he guessed it would be more satisfactory for the seventh grade to use the old route after all.

Dinah Myrtle raised her hand. "Could I go with the seventh grade to lunch?" she asked. "I don't mind the extra walking."

Her classmates laughed, and Alice whispered to Kate, "She wants to get to wave at her boyfriend at the filling station."

"I think it would be best if you stayed with your own grade," said Mr. Bronson.

"But I'm afraid of the ferocious bull!" said Dinah Myrtle as if she really were, and Mr. Bronson consented for her to walk to lunch with the seventh grade.

"And now there's something more important that I want to discuss with you. It has to do with cotton. You don't have to be reminded that the economy of our region is based on farming, and the main crop, of course, is cotton. It's ready to be picked now, but unfortunately, many men are away in service or working in factories. As you know, there's a war on."

Kate wondered how he thought anybody could help but know it. "In any event," continued Mr. Bronson, "the farmers are running into difficulty harvesting their crop, and some of their families may have to stay out of school to help."

"The Poes are out already," said Alex.

"Yes," agreed his father. "The Poes are taken out of school every fall, but this year there may be others—unless something can be done."

Alice whispered to Kate, "Maybe they're going to close school the way Ivy says they do in some places."

At last Mr. Bronson got to the point of his announcement. The Board of Education had declared Tuesday of the following week a holiday with the hope that everyone would help the farmers. If all went well, there would be other days when school would close for the same purpose. Farm children, he knew, would work at home on Tuesday, but he hoped the town students would help too. "The longer cotton stays in the field after it's ready to be picked, the more it depreciates in value. It begins to get dirty and doesn't sell for as high a price." He said that faculty members were urged to pick cotton too. "Of course, you youngsters may be able to do a better job of it than we adults since you don't have to bend over as far to reach the stalks." Putting his hands on the small of his back, he grimaced as if the thought of picking cotton made his back ache. "But I plan to work somewhere. After all, there's a war on."

There he goes again, thought Kate. She'd bet that before he was

74

finished he would say it another time or two and probably mention "our men in uniform" and "the duration" besides. But she was wrong. He ended the meeting, and the sixth grade returned to its own hut.

Before settling back to lessons, Dudley asked if a session of the House of Representatives could be held, and Miss Jordan said that it was all right.

"Anybody got anything to say before I bring up an idea I've had?" asked Dudley.

"Yeah," said Tubby. "I make a motion that we declare Ferdinand a war hero."

Everyone laughed except Ivy. "He can't be a war hero when he's not in the war."

"Like your brother," said Oscar. "We know!"

Miss Jordan said, "There can be heroes at home too. Maybe we could declare the calf a home-front hero."

Kate asked, "What about calling him a wartime home-front hero?"

"Very good!" said Miss Jordan. "I'm for it!" Dudley asked who else was in favor, and everyone's hand went up, including Ivy's.

Then Dudley got to his idea. "It's about next Tuesday and us being off from school," he said. "I guess all of you who live in the country will have to help your own folks pick cotton, won't you?"

"I will," said Winnie Owens; and Melvin Attaway said, "I'm sure I will." All the students from the country agreed that they would be expected to help at home.

"But the ones of us who live in town won't have any special work to do," said Dudley, "and I was wondering if we couldn't go help the Poes. That way maybe Zack and Tootie could come back to school sooner."

Melvin said, "In that case, I'm glad I've got to help at home. Mr. Poe is mean." He emphasized "mean." Melvin and his family lived near the Poes.

"Well, we wouldn't be doing it to help him," said Dudley. "We'd be doing it to help Zack and Tootie."

"I favor it," said Kate. "It's a good idea."

Soon everyone had agreed that it was a fine idea, and the town students decided they would bring their lunches and stay all day at the Poes. But how would they get there? "We could walk," said Kate, "It's only two miles."

Dinah Myrtle said, "I couldn't walk two miles!"

"You could walk a hundred," said Glenn, "if you thought you'd see one of your boyfriends leaning up against a gas pump!"

Miss Jordan said, "Maybe all of you would have more energy to use working if you didn't have to walk quite that distance. What about the train? Isn't Two-Mile Crossing near the Poes' farm?"

"It's right at it," said Dudley.

"My dad goes past Two-Mile Crossing on his way to work," said Alice. "And he goes in his pickup truck. He'd be glad to take us if everybody could be at our house by seven o'clock."

The town students decided they could, and Sylvia Gage asked, "What about you, Miss Jordan? Will you pick with us? Mr. Bronson wants teachers to help."

"No," said Miss Jordan. "I'm sorry, but I can't go with you. There's something that I urgently need to see about in Atlanta, and Tuesday will give me the opportunity to do it."

"What is it you need to see about?" asked Nola May.

"Perhaps I'll tell you after a few weeks. Meanwhile I think it's good that so many of you are willing to help Zack and Tootie."

"We'll pick lots of cotton," said Dudley. "*Operation Cotton Picking*—that's what we'll call it," and the Speaker of the House sat down and the history lesson began.

Operation
Cotton Picking

MEN USUALLY picked cotton with giant burlap bags strapped over their shoulders. Women and children used smaller ones of burlap or cloth. The town students who met in Alice King's yard on Tuesday morning each brought a bag from home. Straps for them ranged from bands of plain cloth, pieces of rope, and strips of canvas to more original materials. Tubby's was a pair of his father's suspenders, and Sylvia had used an old necktie.

All the bags had once contained chicken feed or flour—except Alice's. It was a ragged pillowcase. Dudley teased her. "I'll bet you'll be the only person in the world who ever picked cotton in a sack with lace on it!"

Alice laughed, pulling at the lace trim. "Mamma would have taken it off to use again, but it's beginning to fall apart."

Just then her father came out of the house. "All set?" he asked, counting the boys and girls. "Ten in all, is that the crowd?"

"Yes, sir," answered Dudley. "That's us!"

"The town brigade!" said Mr. King, and everybody began climbing onto the back of the pickup truck. As he drove off, he put his head out of the window and called, "Don't stand up and move around, or you'll fall."

Kate had always enjoyed riding in the back of a truck; there was something about it that gave her a feeling that was not like anything else. Occasionally she had seen dogs leaning out of automobiles, their heads facing into the wind. She believed she knew how it made them feel—free and good. She wondered if dogs had missed riding as much as she had since gas rationing began.

Mr. King had not told his riders to keep quiet, and Kate supposed he didn't mind the noise. Otherwise he'd have asked them to make less of it. They yelled and waved at everyone along the way and soon were at Two-Mile Crossing. "Have a good day," said Mr. King, leaving them on the roadside. "And behave yourselves!"

Glenn asked, "Why do grown-ups always say 'Behave yourselves'?"

"Because they think we need reminding of it, I guess," said Alice as if Glenn had been criticizing her father.

"Anyway all of them don't say it," said Kate.

"No," said Ivy, "Some say, 'Be good!'"

"Yeah," agreed Alex, "and some say, 'Don't get into anything!'"

"How about 'You be sweet now!'?" added Ivy.

"Yes, and 'Act nice, do you hear?'" said Dudley.

Heading toward the cotton field, they began using other expressions they believed adults used too often: "Be careful!" "Don't cause anybody any trouble!" "Remember your manners!"

Tootie was in the corner of the field, nearing the end of a row of cotton. She greeted her friends: "I saw Melvin Attaway on

Sunday, and he told me you were coming. But I didn't believe him!"

Alice said, "We thought we'd get here before you started to work."

Tootie laughed. "You'd have to be here by sunrise to do that!"

"Here," said Tubby, "let's get going!" He picked two bolls of cotton and put them in his sack.

"Let's do," said Alex.

"You don't start just anywhere," said Nathan. "Do you, Tootie?"

"No, you'd better not skip around. But you oughta see Pa before you do anything." Motioning toward the end of the field, she said, "That's him down there near Zack."

When the group reached him, Mr. Poe asked, "What's all this?" He sounded cross.

Everyone waited for someone else to answer. Finally Dudley said, "We've come to help you pick cotton."

"I've got my own children to do the work," said Mr. Poe. "That's what they're for."

Zack put his sack of cotton down and came to speak to his friends. After everyone had greeted him, Dudley asked Mr. Poe, "Won't you let us pick?"

"No! I ain't gonna pay nobody to do work that my own crowd can do."

"But we don't want you to pay us. We just want to help."

Ivy added, "We want to work so Zack and Tootie can come back to school."

"It ain't nobody's business but mine how long they stay out of school," said Mr. Poe, and some of the girls and boys stepped backward as if they would be glad to go home at once.

Kate and Dudley did not back away. "Please, won't you let us help?" asked Kate; and Dudley said, "We'll work if you'll let us." Looking around at all the cotton that was to be picked, he added, "We hoped you'd be glad to see us."

Mr. Poe didn't look as if he were glad to see them, but he did finally say, "Well, all right then, go ahead and pick. Just don't skip over any, and don't drop a bit on the ground, do you hear?"

"Yes, sir," chorused the group.

"When dirt gets in cotton, it gins out sorry and don't bring a decent price. And our living depends on the crop. So I'm warning you, don't get dirt in any of it!"

"We won't," promised Tubby.

"And when you pick a sackful, empty it at the edge of the field on that spread." He pointed toward a giant square of canvas stretched out on the ground. "Zack, get them started on a row apiece, but make haste! We ain't got all day." At that he bent over and went back to work.

Zack led the way to the end of the field. As soon as he was certain that everyone had a row—and that no rows were skipped —he returned to work too.

At first the picking was fun. The cotton was soft to the touch and pleasant, and it weighed so little that even a sackful was not heavy to carry. And the sunshine was warm, instead of scorching hot the way it would have been in midsummer.

Zack brought a bucket of water, and everybody had a drink from a gourd dipper. Then he returned to work, but his friends were slower in starting back. "I think I've picked long enough," said Sylvia. "I'm tired."

Most of them laughed at her, but a few minutes later Dinah

Myrtle said that she was tired too, and she and Sylvia went over and sat in the shade of a big poplar at the edge of the field. Soon Ivy and Alice joined them, and not long afterward all the boys except Dudley stopped to rest. Kate and Dudley worked until their backs began to hurt; then they stopped and joined their classmates in the shade.

Zack and Tootie did not stop to rest, but when their rows of cotton led them near the poplar, they chatted with everyone about Hut School, wanting to hear what had happened since they'd been away. They worked and talked until they were too far away for conversation to continue. Then Kate and Dudley convinced everyone else it was time to pick more cotton.

At twelve o'clock the work stopped. The students from town sat beneath the poplar to eat their lunch. Kate invited Tootie to eat with her, and Dudley offered to share his lunch with Zack, but the twins said they would have to eat with their family.

After finishing lunch, the pickers from town walked to the Poes' house for a fresh drink of water. While they were in the yard, Mrs. Poe came to the back door and threw scraps to a flock of chickens. When she saw the children at the well, she said, "I'm sorry we didn't have dinner enough to share, but I churned this morning, and there's lots of buttermilk if any of you would care for a glass of it."

The children giggled, but no one answered until Dudley said, "Thank you. I don't guess any of us want a glass of it." Tubby whispered, "Buttermilk!" and pretended to heave. His classmates laughed, and Mrs. Poe looked embarrassed as she turned and went back inside. Kate thought about her during the afternoon, and once when she and Tootie were working near each other, she said, "Your mother's nice."

"She was wishing she had something good to offer everybody for refreshments," said Tootie. "She wanted to send to the store for lemons to make a lemonade, but she knew Pa wouldn't allow it. And besides we don't have sugar to spare—with it being rationed and all."

Kate straightened up. "There's a war on!" she said, and both of them laughed. She stretched a moment, but Tootie continued picking and was out of talking range when Kate started back to work.

In midafternoon when Tootie started to the house to get a bucketful of fresh water, Kate said, "I'll go too."

"If you don't mind going," said Tootie, "then I'll get back to work. Pa would think we're playing if it took two of us to fetch water."

Kate went to the house by herself. In the yard she left the bucket by the well and tapped on the back door. Mrs. Poe opened it. She had a baby in her arms. "Yes?"

"I was thinking I would have a glass of the buttermilk if you've still got it to spare."

Mrs. Poe's face brightened. "Why, sure, honey, come on in." Kate stepped into the room that was both kitchen and dining room. "Have a seat!" said Mrs. Poe, motioning toward a straight chair with a bottom made of twisted corn shucks.

"Thank you, but I'd better not sit down or I might not be able to get up again!"

Mrs. Poe laughed. "Picking cotton affects my back that same way!" She poured a glassful of buttermilk and handed it to Kate. "It's good of all of you to come help. Maybe my young 'uns will get back to school earlier on account of it." When Kate didn't say anything, Mrs. Poe continued, "I know that education is im-

83

portant." She forced a laugh and added, "I don't have any of it myself, but I want my children to take as much of it as they can get."

Kate decided that the best way to drink buttermilk was the way she downed medicine—in one gulp. She turned up the glass and drank the milk as fast as she could.

"Have some more, honey," said Mrs. Poe.

"Oh, no, ma'am," said Kate emphatically. "But thank you anyway."

"You must be Kate Coleman."

Kate was surprised. "Yes, ma'am, that's right."

"I've heard Tootie speak of you. I used to know your mama's folks a long time ago. Warn't she a Prescott?"

"Yes, ma'am."

I knowed her when I was a girl," said Mrs. Poe, "but I don't recollect ever making the acquaintance of your pa. Was he from around here?"

"No, ma'am," said Kate. "He lived in Atlanta and didn't move to Redhill till he got married. I'm sorry you don't know him."

Mrs. Poe smiled. "I'm sure I'd like him."

"Everybody does," said Kate as she started back to the well.

In the field, after drinking a gourdful of water, Sylvia said that she was not going back to work. "I just think I'll keel over dead if I bend over one more time."

"I think I will too," said Alice, "but I'll try a while longer anyway." But it was not long until all the girls except Kate had stopped for the day.

After a while, Brewster Poe, who had taken a load of cotton to the gin in town, returned to the farm and started picking cotton. It was Brewster who had joined the Navy at fifteen. He was a year older now, and when Dinah Myrtle saw him, she said she believed her back felt better than it had. She started picking cotton again, but when Brewster had to go on another errand for his father, her back began to bother her, and she returned to the shade of a tree.

Soon Mr. Poe told Tootie and Zack to go to the house to see about their chores before it began getting dark. He told everyone else that it was quitting time and for them to go ahead home. He reminded them to empty what cotton was in their sacks onto the spread at the end of the field.

At the big pile of cotton Alice said, "It looks like a giant cloud!"

"And I'm an airplane flying over it," said Glenn. At that he spread his arms out as if he were flying. Then he leaped into the air, landing on his belly in the center of the pile.

Tubby said, "Move out of the way, Glenn, and watch me do a swan dive!" He took a running start and leaped into the air, landing on the cotton. Soon all the boys and Kate were jumping onto the pile, diving and turning somersaults. Cotton scattered each time, great heaps of it spilling over the edge of the canvas onto the ground.

There was a clap of thunder, and Alice suggested they run to the front porch of the house and wait for her father there.

"What? And drink buttermilk?" asked Tubby, and everybody laughed except Kate. The buttermilk joke wasn't funny now, but playing in the cotton was great. At the same time she knew they shouldn't be doing it.

"Hey, the cotton has scattered," said Nathan, and he and Kate began picking it up and throwing it back onto the pile. When some of it that Nathan had thrown hit Tubby in the face, Tubby laughed and threw a handful at Dudley. "A cotton battle!" cried

Glenn, and soon everyone was throwing it till a cloudburst sent them scurrying for shelter. They ran to the little shed that was the railroad's waiting station for Two-Mile Crossing. As soon as the rain ended, they returned to the field.

There had been just enough rain to wet the top of the soil. Kate felt it sticking to the soles of her shoes as she walked over and picked up a handful of cotton from the ground. She threw the cotton back onto the pile. Stained by the wet soil, it contrasted sharply with the cotton that had not been scattered. The sight of it caused everybody to realize at the same time that they were in trouble. "What can we do?" asked Ivy.

Tubby said, "Let's gather up what's on the ground and hide it underneath the rest."

"Mr. Poe will find out about it," said Dudley. He looked at the mess and shook his head.

Sylvia said, "Well, it's not our fault that it rained."

"It's our fault that we scattered the pile," said Kate, starting to pick up more of the cotton. Ivy and Dudley had begun helping her just as Mr. Poe returned in an empty wagon to collect the cotton.

"What's going on?" he asked, and he saw for himself.

"We're picking it up," said Dudley, his voice a bit shaky.

Nobody else said anything. Mr. Poe stood there, and his face turned a deep red. Kate thought he was going to explode. At last he said, "There's more on the ground than on the spread!" He held up a handful. "And besides getting dirt in it, the mud's stained it." Then he looked at the town brigade. "Get out!" he yelled. "Get out!"

"We're supposed to wait for my daddy to pick us up," said Alice.

"Wait down the road!" said Mr. Poe. "I don't want you in my field." He started gathering up the spilled cotton, and everyone but Kate and Dudley left quickly.

Kate asked, "Can't we help you pick it up?"

"Get out, I said!" shouted Mr. Poe, and Kate and Dudley hurried away.

Facing
Mr. Poe

EVEN GUPPY and Whale looked tired, thought Kate. She was sitting near the window, trying to think of five sentences using pronouns, but it was hard to concentrate. Staring at Guppy, who appeared to be staring back, she said to herself, "He looks dumb." She realized that what she'd said contained a pronoun, and quickly she wrote the sentence, underlining *he*. Then she wrote: "2. *His* friend is Whale. 3. *She* is a fish." Kate didn't know if Whale was a female or not, but it gave her a different pronoun. "4. *They* live in a bowl and say, 'Glub, glub, glub.' 5. *That* means—" and she started to put that it meant "I love you," but she doubted that fish went around saying "I love you," so she looked at Guppy and Whale and tried to guess what they were saying. Her last sentence became "*That* means 'When do we eat?' "

She went back to thinking about yesterday, and she supposed that everyone was thinking about it. The town brigade had told classmates about scattering Mr. Poe's cotton, but no one had mentioned it to Miss Jordan. She was as cheerful as usual.

During the afternoon Dinah Myrtle asked her, "Did you have a good time in Atlanta yesterday?"

Miss Jordan smiled. "Well, yes, I really did."

Nola May asked, "Did you see about whatever it was that you were going to see about?"

"Yes, and I finished early enough to go to a picture show before catching the train back to Redhill. Would you like to hear about it?"

"Oh, yes, ma'am," said Nola May. "We've been wondering what it was you were seeing about."

Miss Jordan smiled again. "No, I mean would you like to hear about the picture show? All of you seem a bit tired, and anyway we've studied enough for today. I was thinking of reading to you."

"We'd rather hear about the picture show that you saw," said Winnie.

"My cousin saw one last week," said Hope. "It was called *Swing-Shift Maisie* and was about this girl who gets a job in an aircraft factory and falls in love with a handsome test pilot. My cousin said it was real funny."

Winnie asked Miss Jordan, "Was Betty Grable in the one you saw? I like picture shows when there's lots of singing and dancing."

"No, Betty Grable wasn't in it. This was a dramatic war story called *First Comes Courage,* and I felt better after seeing it."

"My cousin thought about going to it," said Hope, "but she heard it was sad. How can you feel better after seeing something sad?"

"Well, sometimes stories of other people's courageous deeds can make us feel stronger, don't you think?" Without waiting for an answer, she began telling the story of *First Comes Courage.* It was about a woman from Norway who married within the enemy's territory to try to save her country even though her heart was somewhere else. She suffered a great deal when her motives were mistaken by her friends. When Miss Jordan finished the story, it was time for school to be out.

The next day everybody was in better spirits, but Hut School was still not the same. The sixth graders had whispered among themselves about the trouble they had caused Mr. Poe, but still they had not told Miss Jordan. Then early Friday morning, just as the arithmetic lesson was starting, Miss Jordan said, "I hope some of you told Zack and Tootie how we're moving along; maybe they'll try to keep up with us on their own. Do any of you know when they'll be back? Surely your helping them will make a difference."

At that, Alice blurted out, "We may have hurt their chances of coming back more than we helped them." Then everyone began explaining what had happened. Kate was glad the story was out at last.

After Miss Jordan had listened to the explanations, she said, "Well, I'm sorry. But you're sorry too, and of course you shouldn't have done it, but you'll be more careful next time."

"Let's help the Poes again next time!" said Alice. "When will we have another day off to pick cotton?"

"Aw, ol' Mr. Poe won't let us on his farm again," said Tubby. "Remember how he ran us off?"

"Anyway," said Miss Jordan, "I don't think school will be closed again. Mr. Bronson told me that the board had decided against it."

Sylvia said, "Then we couldn't help Zack and Tootie even if ol' Mr. Poe would allow us back on his property."

Kate spoke up, "We could help them on a Saturday."

There was immediate silence. Everyone looked shocked that

anyone could have come up with such a silly idea. Eventually Glenn asked, "Are you crazy?"

"No, I'm not crazy," said Kate angrily.

"Now let's be calm—" said Miss Jordan, "and democratic. Dudley, if you'll step forward and preside we'll turn this into a session of the House of Representatives." She went to the back of the room, and Dudley went to the front.

"Anybody got anything to bring up?" he asked.

"Yes," said Kate. "I want to propose that all of us from town, and anyone else who doesn't have work to do at home, offer to help the Poes tomorrow."

"But tomorrow's Saturday," said Dudley.

"And I propose we help them," insisted Kate.

Tubby said, "You're out of your mind all right, Kate. If we can't have a day off from school, I sure ain't gonna work on a Saturday."

"Me neither," said Alex.

Dinah Myrtle said, "I always have to wash my hair on Saturday and roll it up and polish my fingernails and other things."

"What other things do you polish?" asked Dudley, and everybody laughed.

"Oh, silly, I mean I have to do other things to get ready for my Saturday night date."

Sylvia said, "I'm supposed to go over to my aunt's house tomorrow. She's been saving her sugar ration for us to make cookies and candy to send to soldiers. We have to try to keep up the morale of our men in uniform."

Oscar groaned. "*Our men in uniform!*"

Nathan said, "I'm supposed to tear down a tree house that Mamma says spoils the looks of our front yard."

Other reasons were given why Saturday was not a good day to work at the Poes, and Dudley asked Kate, "Do you want to take back your suggestion?"

"No," said Kate, firmly. "We got ourselves into trouble, and we should get ourselves out!"

Tubby, imitating Dinah Myrtle, said, "But I've got to roll up my hair!"

Everybody laughed, but soon they were serious again. Dudley said, "Well, all right, I'm willing to work tomorrow if anybody else is."

"I am," said Alice. "Back-breaking as the work is, I'd rather do it than worry any longer about what we did."

"Well," said Nathan, "since the tree house has been in the yard since last summer, I guess it can stay a little longer."

Soon all the town students had agreed that they would work. Melvin Attaway and Winnie Owens, who lived on farms near the Poes, said there was a possibility that they might not have to work at home on Saturday afternoon, in which case they would help part of the day.

"But somebody'll have to ask Mr. Poe if he'll let us," said Dudley. "Who'll do it?"

Nobody volunteered till Kate said, "All right, I'll go if somebody'll go with me."

Dudley waited. When no one spoke up, he said, "O.K., I'll go with you."

"Me too," said Alex. "And, say, it's nearly time for the train! If we hurry, we could catch it to Two-Mile Crossing."

"But how would you get back?" asked Miss Jordan.

"We could walk—or run!"

Miss Jordan looked at her watch. "I suppose we should clear it with your father, but then you'd miss the train, so go ahead. After all, there's a war on!"

Kate, Dudley, and Alex got to the station just as the train was starting to pull out. Mr. Wilson had not closed the door to the last passenger car, and he helped them climb aboard as the train inched along, getting up steam. Fare for children going such a short distance was ten cents, he said, but if they didn't have it he would let them ride free. Kate had thirteen cents, and Dudley asked to borrow the three cents she had left over to go with his nickel, plus two pennies he borrowed from Alex, who had a quarter. By the time all the change was figured, they were almost to Two-Mile Crossing. Mr. Wilson pulled the chain that was a signal to the engineer. Unless someone wanted to get off the train at the crossing, or unless someone flagged it to a halt for boarding, it did not stop.

Soon the three sixth graders were walking across the field where the entire Poe family was at work. "Mrs. Poe's with them," said Alex.

Kate said, "Tootie told me her mother helps in the field whenever she's caught up on her housework—and when the baby's napping. She said Mr. Poe used to make her bring the baby to the field and leave it at the end of a row on a quilt, but one day there was a poisonous snake nearby when they got back to it, and Mrs. Poe has refused to bring the baby to the field anymore. She goes back to the house real often to check on it, or else she sends Tootie."

They were near the Poes then, and Dudley lowered his voice. "Don't Mr. Poe look ferocious? Maybe we shouldn't be here!"

"Let's turn around and run!" suggested Alex.

Kate was wishing they hadn't come, but when she saw Zack

and Tootie smiling at them, she was not about to turn back. Soon she was facing Mr. Poe, and when neither of the boys said anything, she told him, "We've come to ask you something."

"Yeah?" growled Mr. Poe.

"But first we want to tell you how sorry we are about what happened on Tuesday."

"Yes, sir," said Dudley. "We sure are sorry."

"Yes, sir," echoed Alex. "We sure are."

"And we want to try to make up for it," continued Kate. "If you'll let us, we'll work for you tomorrow."

"No," said Mr. Poe, but at least he didn't shout it—or shake his fist when he said it.

"There'd be lots of us again," said Dudley.

"And we'd work all day," added Alex.

"You didn't pick much cotton before," said Mr. Poe.

"Now, Pa," said Mrs. Poe, "they picked a sight of it."

"Well, they messed it up after they picked it—and what we picked besides."

"We won't mess up anything again," said Dudley. "We promise not to."

"Yes, sir," said Alex, "we promise not to."

Tootie spoke up. "Let 'em help us, Pa. We won't ever get all this done by ourselves."

Brewster, who had walked over from where he had been picking, made a sweeping gesture to take in the acres of cotton still in the field. "If you won't let somebody help us, it's gonna stay out here till it gins out sorry anyhow."

Mr. Poe said nothing for a moment. He spit tobacco juice onto the ground, and then stared at where he'd spit. At last he said, "Well, all right. But if airy one of you act up, I'll take a stick and drive you off the place, do you hear?"

"Yes, sir," said Kate. He'd said it so loud that nobody could have helped hearing. "Thank you," she said, and she and Dudley and Alex left before he could change his mind.

They hurried back to town and were almost to the two big houses in front of Hut School when they saw Mr. Bledsoe, the town marshal, in the Redhill police car. He came out of the driveway between the two houses. As he turned into the main road, they saw that a girl was with him.

"That was Ivy!" said Dudley as if he couldn't believe it. "What do you suppose she's done wrong?"

"Must be something terrible," said Alex, "for Mr. Bledsoe to get her out of school. Come on, I'll race you!"

He was ahead three steps when he declared a race underway, but Dudley and Kate passed him before they reached the hut. "What's happened?" asked Dudley, rushing into the class.

"Was Ivy arrested?" asked Kate.

Miss Jordan looked worried. "I don't know what's happened," she said, "but I doubt that Ivy's done anything wrong. Mr. Bledsoe said that her family asked him to come for her." She allowed the discussion to continue for a few moments; then she helped the town students make plans for the following day. They were to meet at Alice's house again and catch a ride with her father. "What about you, Miss Jordan?" asked Sylvia. "Will you pick with us?"

"I'm afraid not," said Miss Jordan, "I have to go to Atlanta."

"What for?" asked Nola May.

"I have to take some tests," answered Miss Jordan, and then she looked as if she hadn't meant to say it. "I mean, I have to see about several things, and it's necessary for me to be away tomorrow."

Tests? thought Kate. *A grown woman taking tests? Arithmetic?*

English? Georgraphy? Then she remembered another kind of tests. Her mother sometimes mentioned people who took medical tests in Atlanta when local doctors couldn't find out what was wrong with them. Sometimes bad things were the matter when Redhill doctors put anybody to the trouble of going somewhere else for examinations. Mrs. Pinson, a lady who had lived near the Colemans, had gone into Atlanta for tests; Kate heard her mother and Mrs. Shaw talking about it. The next news she'd heard was that Mrs. Pinson had died.

War News

"Looks like they'd at least call his name on the air!" said Kate as the news report came to an end.

"Is that why you've been listening?" asked her father, turning off the radio. "Kaltenborn comments on national news. Anything that happens to Georgians is more likely to be reported by a local announcer."

"Well, it ought to be on national news," insisted Kate.

"Yes, of course, but if every casualty were announced, there wouldn't be time for anything else."

It was not until after school that Kate learned why the Holbrooks had asked Mr. Bledsoe to bring Ivy home. They had received a telegram from the War Department, and they wanted her to hear of it from them. Otherwise, the way news traveled in a small town, she might have heard about it on the way home, with no one to console her. The telegram had reported that Marcus Holbrook had been killed.

Mrs. Coleman held out a section of the *Atlanta Journal*. "Here's a short piece about Marcus in tonight's paper."

Kate took the newspaper and read the article to her father:

In a telegram to Mr. and Mrs. Clayton Holbrook, of Redhill, the War Department revealed that their son, Marcus, had been killed in action in the Southwest Pacific war zone.

Marcus was all-state quarterback at Waycross during high school days and had been offered athletic scholarships to several colleges prior to his enlistment. He is survived by his parents and two sisters, Ivy and Maxine.

Kate folded the paper and put it on a chair. "Ivy told us he was a football hero."

"Now he's a dead hero," said Mr. Coleman, and nobody spoke for a long time. Then he said, "Maybe we should go over to see the Holbrooks."

"They've gone to Waycross for a few days," said Mrs. Coleman. "They lived there before they moved to Redhill, and most of their people are down there."

Kate told her parents about the way Ivy spoke often of her brother being in service. "But we didn't listen half the time because she talked about him so much. Somebody always butted in and stopped her."

"Well, I hope it wasn't you," said her mother.

Kate thought for a moment. Had she been the one to tell Ivy to quit talking about her brother? "No," she said, "it wasn't me. I got tired of hearing about him sometimes, and I might have spoken up, but usually it was Oscar Yates who'd stop her. He'd tell her that nobody wanted to keep hearing it and that people are needed at home to help win the war too."

"Which indeed they are," said Mr. Coleman, "but it's interesting that the Yates boy should be the one to say so." Mrs. Coleman nodded, and Kate sensed there was something her parents weren't telling her. She asked what it was.

Her mother said, "Oh, nothing really"; but Mr. Coleman explained, "Oscar's older brother has been criticized for staying out of service to help run his father's cattle farm."

"Farmers can get deferred," said Kate.

"But it seems he wasn't a farmer till the draft got in behind him; he'd been working in Savannah. Yet maybe he's needed to help his old man now. Who knows?"

Mrs. Coleman said sternly, "But Kate, you'll forget you heard it mentioned. Do you hear?"

Mr. Coleman answered for Kate, "Of course she will. Kate knows that some things we tell are not to be discussed at school."

"What about you?" Kate asked.

Her father laughed. "Me? Well, I don't go to school, but I guess I realize that families discuss matters at times that aren't meant for conversations outside the home."

"No," said Kate. "I was talking about the draft. Would you go if you were called?"

"I can let you know if I'm called," said Mr. Coleman. "I never say what I would or wouldn't do in someone else's place. If I were the Yates boy, for instance, I suppose I'd do exactly what he's done. Otherwise I wouldn't be him, would I?"

"You won't really be called, will you?" asked Kate.

"Why, I'd imagine the Army would look on me as a hindrance!" When Kate didn't laugh, he added, "On the other hand, there are not many single men left to be drafted."

Mrs. Coleman said, "A lot of the married ones who don't have any children have been called into the service too."

Mr. Coleman looked at her. "I've been meaning to tell you. The draft boards in some counties have already sent notices to men with children."

"Pre-Pearl Harbor?" asked Mrs. Coleman. Kate knew that meant, "Did they have children before the war began?" which gave them a different status in the draft from recent fathers.

"Yes, pre-Pearl Harbor," said her father.

"Oh, no!" said Mrs. Coleman.

"Well, you and Kate would get along fine without me."

Kate said emphatically, "No, we wouldn't!" She could not imagine having to get along without her father.

Mr. Coleman laughed. "You and your mother look so gloomy at the mere mention of it, I don't think I'll tell you if I'm ever drafted. Otherwise you'll depress me to death with your long faces before I can take my turn at being shot at by the enemy!" When neither of them said anything, he went on teasing. "If I'm drafted, I may just wait until I'm already at some Army camp way off in a swamp. Then I'll write you a post card saying, 'Having a mushy time. Wish you were here.'"

"You'll tell me just as soon as you receive your notice!" said Mrs. Coleman.

"No! If I tell you, you'll mope, and Kate will mope, and I'll go away remembering you as a couple of mopers!"

Kate laughed, but Mrs. Coleman said, "You'll remember me as your *ex*-wife if you go away without telling me!"

"We're crossing bridges before we get to them," said Mr. Coleman. Turning the radio back on, he added, "And we're about to fool around and miss 'The Thin Man.'"

"Yes, let's listen," said Mrs. Coleman. "And 'The Playhouse' is next. John Garfield's in a play called *Fallen Sparrow*."

Kate started to say that she would rather hear "Gang Busters," which came on at the same time. But her mother did not have many favorite programs, and anyway Kate liked John Garfield too. It suited her to listen to *Fallen Sparrow*.

Except for Ivy, all the students who had helped the Poes on Tuesday returned on Saturday. As soon as they were in the field they began working, everyone suddenly becoming very quiet.

Tootie said, "You can talk and pick at the same time. Pa won't get mad about that." Some of the boys and girls began to chat then, but they were careful to continue working.

After an hour Sylvia stopped to rest, and soon Dinah Myrtle and Alice stopped too, leaving Kate the only girl from town still working. When Glenn and Tubby decided to quit for a while, they asked if she didn't want to stop too.

"No," said Kate. "I can't help it if I'm able to hold out longer than you are."

At that, Tubby and Glenn went back to picking cotton, saying that no girl could do more work than they could. Kate began working faster then, and the two boys had to hurry to keep up with her. Dudley, Alex, and Nathan were hard at work too, but soon everyone stopped. Kate refused to rest long, however, and everybody went back to work when she did. Only Zack and Tootie had not stopped at all.

At noon the town students sat in the shade of a thicket of sweet gums, avoiding briers that grew there. The ground beneath the big poplar, where they had stopped on Tuesday, was smoother, but it was a distance from where they were now working. Nobody felt energetic enough to walk back to it.

While they were eating, Winnie came along. "I ate before I left home," she said, accepting a sandwich Kate had offered her. "But I'll be sociable."

"Is Melvin coming?" asked Dudley.

"No," said Winnie, motioning in the direction from which she had come. "All the Attaways were in their own field when I came past. I almost had to stay at home and work too, but Pa decided we needed Saturday afternoon off."

"But you'll be working here," said Alice.

"I know," agreed Winnie. "But this is different."

Kate knew that what made it different was being with friends, and she thought about how lonely some jobs must be. She only half-listened to Dinah Myrtle telling about her latest boyfriend. "He's in the tenth grade," said Dinah Myrtle, "and he tried to kiss me last Saturday night, but I told him I didn't believe in kissing on a first date. But maybe if he tries again tonight, I'll kiss him back, especially if he's got his daddy's car and enough gas for us to go to Griffin to a picture show." The Poes came out of their house, ready to return to work, before she could discuss the matter in more detail.

"O.K., everybody, on your feet!" said Dudley.

Kate was so tired that she wasn't sure she could get to her feet —or stand on them. But she made it, sighing with everyone else. Tubby complained the loudest. "I'm in pain!"

"Bend up and down, and you'll get over it," advised Dudley, and soon the town brigaders and Winnie were in the field, each one concentrating on the work to be done.

At the first suggestion of a rest in the afternoon, Kate said, "It's when you stay still and then have to start back that you hurt."

"Let's just stay still and not start back!" said Alice.

"Let's do," said Sylvia.

"No," said Alice, shrugging. "I guess I favor working after all. The more we pick, the more days it'll cut off the time Zack and Tootie have to stay out of school."

By late afternoon Kate had never felt so tired. She doubted that anyone else had either. Even Sylvia, her long, blonde curls wet with perspiration, looked bedraggled. Kate ran her fingers through her own hair. Both hands were dirty, but it didn't matter. Probably by now her hair was coated with so much dust that it was more the color of Georgia's red clay than black anyway.

At quitting time so much cotton had been picked that even Mr. Poe seemed pleased, although he didn't come right out and say so. The nearest he came to thanking them was to say, "You've done all right," as Winnie headed toward a path through the woods that was a shortcut home for her, and the town brigade started toward the road.

"We'll be back next Saturday," said Kate, but partway across the field, Glenn said, "You're nutty as pecan pie, Kate Coleman, if you think I'll work again next Saturday."

Everyone else agreed with him.

Kate, her back aching as if she might never be free of pain, said, "I can't help it if I'm stronger than the rest of you." That made it certain, she knew, that everyone would help the Poes again.

Starting past the big spread where cotton was piled high, Kate thought about the fun of jumping and tumbling in it. Her back might not hurt so much if she could do it again. Without a signal from anyone, the whole brigade stopped.

"I still say it looks like a big, white cloud," said Alice.

"Watch my swan dive!" said Tubby, stepping forward as if he were going to leap into the air.

Dudley grabbed him by one arm and Alex by the other, and the two of them led him from the field.

Everybody else followed, and no one stopped or turned around until they were at the waiting shelter for Two-Mile Crossing. Soon Mr. King would come along in his pickup truck and give them a ride to town.

Last Day
in the Cotton

IVY RETURNED to school at mid-week. She was a few minutes late, and the spelling lesson was underway. Miss Jordan stopped to welcome her. "We've been missing you," she said. "And all of us want you to know how terrible we feel for you." Then she added, talking to everyone, "I've never told any of you this, partly because I haven't wanted to talk about it—or maybe it's that I haven't been able to talk about it—but like Ivy, I had a brother who was killed in service."

She drew a quick breath and did not continue talking immediately.

Kate thought, Maybe that's why she hasn't talked about it; maybe she bursts out crying when she mentions it. But Miss Jordan did not cry. She started again, very slowly at first. "My brother was younger than I. He went into the Navy right out of high school, and later he was assigned to the *Arizona*, a battleship that was sunk in Pearl Harbor the day the war started."

"For the United States," said Nathan. "Part of the world was already at war."

"Yes," agreed Miss Jordan. "The attack on Pearl Harbor brought us into it."

Nola May waved her hand in the air and said, "Pearl Harbor Day was December 7, 1941."

"That's right, and it was almost two years ago, although it seems as if it were much longer." Miss Jordan looked out the window. "Yet there are times when it seems as if it were only yesterday— or that it never happened at all, that it was only a bad dream I had." Then she looked at Ivy. "I've learned that the way to keep from dwelling on sorrow is to stay busy. So quick now, everybody, let's get on with spelling. Maybe it would be fun if we turned today's lesson into a match. What do you say?"

"Fine!" chorused the class.

"All right then, boys on one side of the room and girls on the other. Or would you rather choose sides?"

"Boys against the girls!" said Glenn and Tubby both at the same time while Dinah Myrtle said, "I'd rather choose up."

Miss Jordan said, "Ivy, we'll let you decide."

"Girls against the boys," said Ivy, and the match got underway. Toward the end of it, the girls were far ahead. Three of them— Kate, Alice, and Hope—were still standing when all the boys had been seated except Dudley. He had to spell a word correctly after each of them. Hope missed lizard, spelling it *l-i-z-e-r-d,* and then Alice spelled navigate *n-a-v-e-r-g-a-t-e.* Dudley did not make a mistake on either one.

Kate spelled her next three words correctly, and so did Dudley. Then the word balloon was given. *"B-a-l-o-o-n,"* spelled Kate.

"Sorry!" said Miss Jordan.

"The boys win! Hooray!" shouted Henry.

"Not unless Dudley spells balloon right!" said Sylvia.

"Try it, Dudley," said Miss Jordan.

Kate had no doubt that he'd get it right. The problem had been in knowing whether balloon had two *l*'s or one, and since she'd used only one, Dudley would spell it with two—which is exactly what he did. She'd have been disappointed in him if he hadn't.

"Too bad!" said Winnie Owens when Kate sat down, "but next time we'll kill 'em!" Everybody laughed because Winnie was always the first one to have to sit down in a spelling match.

Georgraphy was next, and Miss Jordan helped everyone locate the main cities in Italy that had been in the war news recently.

Soon it was recess, and outside Kate noticed that no one talked to Ivy about her brother's death, but everyone was especially nice to her—even Oscar. Kate wondered if he felt a bit ashamed that he had always been the one to complain when Ivy had talked about her brother. He looked sheepish—or maybe she only imagined it. She knew that no one really blamed him for his comments to Ivy, because almost everyone had felt as he had. But maybe he was being harsh on himself and felt that he had been cruel. She thought of what her father had said about being in someone else's place and tried to think how she would feel if she were Oscar. She believed she would feel badly, and when he stood off to himself while everyone else gathered around to look at a terrapin Melvin had found, she thought of going up to him and saying, "I've put myself in your place, Oscar, and I know how you feel." But that might not have made sense to him, and if she tried to explain, possibly she would have made him feel worse. She decided instead that she would be considerate of him in some other way, so she called on him during arithmetic, when it was her turn to ask questions and she was certain that he knew the answers. Also she proposed him as the one to take a message to Mr. Bronson when no one could agree on whose turn it was.

But Oscar took advantage of her generosity when he pushed into line in front of her and Winnie when they were starting into the lunchroom. The boys liked to be last in line for the walk from Hut School to the gymasium, but sometimes they tried to move to the head of it when they got there. Kate and Winnie promptly shoved Oscar aside, Winnie giving him a whack on the head with her knuckles. Everyone back of them laughed and stood closer together. Oscar would have had to go to the end of the line if Dudley and Alex hadn't let him break into it just ahead of them.

In the afternoon Kate decided that everybody was concerned about Ivy during school and that she should do something special for her after school. Maybe she and Dudley could help keep Ivy's mind off her brother's death by walking home with her. It was several blocks out of the way for them, but when Dudley agreed that it was a good idea, they convinced Ivy that it would be easier walking than their usual route.

Of course, they didn't usually walk; they ran. But they could run after they had seen Ivy home, so they began walking with her every afternoon. After a few weeks, Alice started walking with them too, and Alex came along sometimes.

One Friday afternoon in early November all of them stopped at the main building of the grammar school to see the new rooms that were being added. Mr. Morgan, the carpenter in charge, was Alice's uncle, and he let them go inside for a closer look.

"Everything seems finished to me," said Alice. "What's lacking?"

"Not much," said Mr. Morgan, fastening a latch onto one of the windows. "Everything'll be done in another day or two."

"I think this is the room we're to have," said Alice.

"Miss Jordan's desk can go right here," said Alice, who was

standing near the front of the room, "and the maps can go on the wall over there."

Ivy said, "And let's put the fish bowl in the second window. Guppy and Whale will like it best."

"O.K.," said Dudley. "But why?"

"Cause it's near the radiator."

Mr. Morgan laughed. "They'd better get near a radiator! Cold weather'll be here before long."

The days were still sunny and warm, but the nights were cool, and the following morning Kate shivered as she got up from the breakfast table. Her mother said, "You really should wear a sweater."

The town brigaders were going to the Poes again. It would be their seventh Saturday in the field. "What if you get out there," asked her father, "and there's no cotton left to be picked?"

"We could play all day," said Kate, and before her mother could comment she added, "Don't worry. Mr. Poe wouldn't let us do that. And anyway Miss Jordan'll be with us."

It was the third Saturday that Miss Jordan had gone with the students.

Whatever tests she had taken in Atlanta had been finished, Kate supposed. If they were medical ones, she must have passed them all right. She was healthy enough to pick cotton, and she worked as hard at it as everyone else.

In the afternoon Miss Jordan took a turn at bringing a bucket of water from the well. When everyone who was thirsty had taken a drink of it, she gave Tootie a dipperful to pour onto Tubby. He had stopped to rest at the end of a row and had fallen asleep, propped against a large rock.

Only a few drops of water touched him, but he yelled as if he were drowning. Everyone was laughing, Tootie most of all as she held the gourd dipper and threatened to dash more water onto Tubby, when Mr. Poe came along.

Immediately there was silence, and Kate was certain that he was going to chase the town brigade away—and maybe take out his anger on Tootie. He did tell them to quit work, but not because he was mad. He said that Mrs. Poe wanted to serve them refreshments before they went home, this being their last Saturday in the field. He said that Zack and Tootie could quit too; the little bit of cotton still in the field could be picked Monday.

Then he went to help Brewster load cotton onto a wagon. He did not thank anyone for all the work that had been done, but Kate guessed he appreciated it. After all, he was letting them celebrate now.

On the way to the house Tubby whispered, "Guess what the refreshments will be?" and then gave his own answer, "Buttermilk!"

"I'll drink it if it is!" said Kate, fearing that Tubby was right, but she need not have worried. Refreshments were big glasses of juice made from wild grapes called muscadines that Tootie and Zack had gathered in the woods. With the grape juice was served delicious cake. It contained nuts and dried fruit that had been produced on the farm. Mrs. Poe brought out a large platter of it for second helpings, saying to each guest, "Have some more cake, honey." Then she said, "Zack and Tootie will be back in school earlier than they usually are, and we sure do thank all of you for helping us."

"You sure are welcome," said Dudley, speaking for everyone but taking more refreshments for himself. "And this sure is good cake!"

"It's divine," said Miss Jordan, "but it must have taken your sugar ration for weeks!"

"Why, it's sweetened with honey, honey," said Mrs. Poe, and

everybody laughed. "Zack found the beehive in a tree down by the spring."

That was all that was needed to start Zack on a tale about how he'd gotten the honey from the hollow tree, outwitting the bees and robbing their hive without wearing a net to keep from being stung. "Those bees thought I was a friend instead of a thief," he concluded.

"Well, you were a friendly thief, honey," said Mrs. Poe, smiling. "You left them enough for their winter too." Then she said that it was time for Zack and Tootie to be seeing to their chores, and Miss Jordan and the town brigade started walking back to Redhill instead of waiting for Alice's father to pick them up.

On the way when Kate and Miss Jordan were walking together, everyone else a distance back of them, Miss Jordan said, "It makes you feel good to have done a job well, doesn't it?"

"Yes, ma'am," said Kate.

"You and Dudley have been great! The two of you worked every Saturday, didn't you?"

"So did Alice," said Kate. "And Ivy only missed once, which was while she was in Waycross." Others in the town brigade had helped some Saturdays and skipped others.

"I realize that everybody has worked," said Miss Jordan, "and I'm not taking away from what anyone else has done, including myself." Laughing, she added, "I'm not sure my back will ever be the same. But still you and Dudley were the leaders, and I just, well, wanted to commend you." Kate didn't say anything, and Miss Jordan continued, "I somehow expect one of you to be President of the United States some day."

"Girls can't be President," said Kate.

"Who knows?" said Miss Jordan. "Maybe when you're grown

they can. And I'll be able to say that I taught you—at least part of a year." Just then a horn blew, and they looked back to see Alice's father stopping in his pickup truck.

While Miss Jordan was getting into the cab of the truck with Mr. King, Kate climbed into the back with her classmates. She was glad to have a ride, but she was sorry the conversation with Miss Jordan had ended. What had she meant by "at least part of a year"?

A Letter from
the South Pacific

MISS JORDAN was surprised on Monday that Zack and Tootie were not back in school.

"There was a little more cotton to be picked today," said Alice.

"Yes, now I remember," said Miss Jordan. But the next day the Poes still had not returned.

Melvin Attaway explained, "There's more work to be done on a farm this time of year, even if the cotton has been picked already. Corn has to be brought in and stored for winter feed, and wheat and oats have to be planted, and sweet potatoes need to be dug. But it won't take long."

At supper Kate suddenly decided that she would help the Poes with the rest of their work, but her parents persuaded her against it. They thought it might be better to let Mr. Poe and his family handle their remaining chores by themselves. "Besides," said Mr. Coleman, "I'm needing you here. We'll soon have spinach and turnip greens and radishes to harvest. And whether we like it or not, your mother will want to do more canning, so we'll have our own picking brigade, you and me."

"Can you can radishes?" asked Kate.

"No," answered Mrs. Coleman, "but turnip greens and spinach are nice for canning. They don't lose too much food value or flavor in the process."

"They don't improve a bit!" added Mr. Coleman, and he and Kate laughed.

"It's too bad about you two," teased Mrs. Coleman. "You'd rather grow good things than eat them!"

"I wish we could grow pineapples and bananas," said Kate, smacking her lips. "They're what I call *good things*."

"I'm afraid we've tasted our last pineapple for the duration," said Mrs. Coleman, "and we won't see bananas very often. But think of families in war-torn countries who don't have enough of anything to eat."

Mr. Coleman refused to be serious. He asked Kate, "How does turnip-green upside-down cake sound to you?"

"Delicious!" said Kate, "and spinach ice cream might be good."

"Yes," agreed her father. "For special occasions, how about a dip of it on a cucumber sliced in two?"

"A cucumber split!" said Kate.

"With some whipped cream on top!"

"With chopped-up string beans over the whipped cream!" added Kate.

"And a radish in the middle!" said Mr. Coleman. Getting up from the table, he patted his stomach. "We're making me hungry again," he said, "or sick! Anyway, Kate, there's work to be done in the old victory garden, and it'll be good to have you here on Saturdays." Giving her a hug as he started past her chair he added, "It's not bad having you here on Tuesdays either."

"Say, that's right," said Kate, "this *is* Tuesday. It'll soon be time for 'Fibber McGee and Molly'!"

"No radio programs till you finish your homework!" said Mrs. Coleman. "I don't believe you studied this afternoon."

"There's no homework for tomorrow," said Kate.

"What?" said her father, pretending to be shocked. "No homework on a week night?"

"Miss Jordan said we'd worked so hard lately that we deserved a night off. Wasn't that nice of her?"

Mr. Coleman laughed. "It sure was—even if she loses her job on account of it!"

"I'll quit school if she loses her job," said Kate angrily.

"Now calm down," said Mrs. Coleman. "She isn't going to lose her job, and you forget you heard your father even say such a thing!"

"She may not lose it," said Mr. Coleman, propping against the sideboard. "But it's a shame that some parents are criticizing her so much that they're apt to drive her off. And it's purely because the kids are enjoying school. I ran into Gus Oliver at the post office yesterday, and he was complaining that his son is having too much fun this year. Gus is convinced the term is being wasted, but I told him that I thought Kate was having a good year."

"I am," said Kate. "So is everybody else."

"He said that he and his wife feel that young what's-his-name is liking school too much to be getting anything out of it."

"*Nathan,*" said Kate, "that's his name. All he used to care about doing was dusting the erasers or feeding the fish, but now he takes an interest in lessons too. He's so carried away with history, on account of Miss Jordan makes it sound as if it really happened, that—"

When her mother and father laughed, she corrected herself. "Well, I know history really happened, but I mean Miss Jordan

118

makes it so exciting that some of us have been reading books about it that we don't have to."

"That's something else Gus said," continued Mr. Coleman. "He said his kid was reading books that weren't even texts, and how did a teacher expect a sixth grader to keep up with his lessons if he was all the time reading books." Mrs. Coleman smiled, and Mr. Coleman continued, "If we'd talked longer I might have had to tell him what dumbbells he and his wife are, but lucky for him, he had to leave about that time." Then he laughed and added, "Or maybe it was lucky for me! Gus is bigger than I am and might have taken a swing at me."

"You could whip him," said Kate. "I'm sure you could! Next time tell him!"

"Now stop it, you two!" said her mother. "And mention of the post office reminds me, I didn't have a chance to pick up our mail today."

"I meant to stop by on the way home," said Mr. Coleman. "Maybe I'll just step up there now and see if there's anything in our box. Want to walk with me, Kate?"

"Sure," said Kate, hopping up from the table; but her mother said, "If you'll help me with the dishes, we'll all be able to hear 'Fibber McGee and Molly.'"

"Couldn't we skip washing dishes tonight?"

"No, but we could skip 'Fibber McGee.'"

"Oh, all right," said Kate; and she and her mother got busy. They had finished the dishes and were listening to the program when Mr. Coleman returned from the post office. Fibber had just started to open the closet door of his house; usually it was one of the funniest things that happened. Whenever the door opened, there was always a noise as if the whole place were falling down.

But it was only the contents of Fibber's closet crashing to the floor.

Mr. Coleman sat down beside Kate to listen to the rest of the program, which Kate thought was better than ever. But she noticed that her father did not laugh the way he usually did.

After the radio had been turned off, Mr. Coleman took the mail from his pocket. There was a bill for electricity from the Georgia Power Company, a post card from an uncle in Richmond, and a letter for Kate. "It's from Marcus Holbrook," said her father.

"Marcus Holbrook?" said Kate, almost shouting it. "But he was killed!" Then she added, "Maybe there was a mistake; maybe he wasn't killed after all."

"No," said Mr. Coleman. "I'm afraid it's just that mail sometimes takes weeks, or even months, to get here from a battle zone." Handing her the letter, he added, "It's probably been in the hold of a ship most of the time since it was written."

Kate opened the letter. "I'll read it out loud," she said; and her parents listened. "It starts 'Dear Kate,' and then it says, 'The letters from you and Ivy were the only ones that came to our unit yesterday, and my buddies said I should pass them around. They know that Ivy is my sister, but they thought you were my girl friend! They were surprised when I let them read both letters, and even the ones who knew that you were a friend of Ivy's said that you didn't write like a little kid.'"

Kate looked up and said indignantly, "I'm not *a little kid.*"

"I should say you're not!" agreed Mr. Coleman as Kate went back to reading. "Thank you for telling me about the songs that are popular at home. You said you would send me the words to some of the new ones if I wanted them. Well, if you know the words to 'I Had the Craziest Dream,' would you mind writing them out for me? I am all the time having dreams, crazy ones, and

someone told me he believed there had been a song by that name. He also told me a joke about another song. It's about 'Paper Doll.' If you haven't heard the joke, here it is. Do you know who the mother of the paper doll is? The answer is, An old bag! Ha! Ha!"

Her parents smiled as Kate continued. "Thank you for writing me. I do not know all of Ivy's friends, but I remember that you are the one with long blonde curls and bright blue eyes. Sincerely yours, Marcus Holbrook."

Mr. Coleman said, "Well, he went to glory picturing you as a pretty blonde!"

"Now, dear!" scolded Mrs. Coleman.

"He went to glory picturing me as Sylvia Gage!" said Kate. At that, she burst out crying. "It's not fair. Everybody remembers Sylvia!"

"Now, now!" said Mrs. Coleman, taking Kate into her arms. "It's all right." Kate was glad she didn't say, "Now stop crying." She knew her mother understood that she was not really crying because Marcus had mistaken her for Sylvia, although she wished he hadn't, but because he had been killed. Someone who had written to her had been killed before the letter even reached her—someone who was the brother of a friend of hers right here in Redhill, who had answered her letter as if he were a friend too. Then she realized that her mother was crying with her, and her father was sitting by them.

After a few moments Kate stood up. "I'm going to my room," she said, starting away. Thoughts about war crowded into her mind and tried to sort themselves out, but all she could think to say was, "And I know all the words to 'I Had the Craziest Dream.'"

Miss Jordan's
News

THE TENTH DAY of November
was the last day of Hut School. "We're moving!" said Miss Jordan. "Mr. Bronson will come for us this morning."

"Let's play outside till time to go," suggested Dudley.

"Yeah, let's do!" said Tubby.

Everyone looked at Miss Jordan. After a moment she said, "Cold gray days are ahead of us. Why don't we go outside while there's sunshine?"

"Are you saying that we can have recess already?" asked Nola May.

"Unless you'd rather work," said Miss Jordan; and Nola May answered "Oh, no, ma'am," as she raced outside with everyone else.

The class kept to the side of the hut away from the seventh grade and did not go back inside until midmorning. The English lesson had started, and Henry was insisting that the sentence, "Three chickens flew away," contained three nouns when Mr. Bronson arrived.

"Now if each of you will carry your own belongings," said Mr. Bronson, "we'll have you back in the main building in no time!"

"You mean, *now?*" asked Oscar.

"Yes, now!" said Mr. Bronson, picking up a vase and a paper-weight from a table in the corner. "And what about some help with Miss Jordan's things?"

All the boys rushed to the front of the room. "I get to take the globe!" said Oscar, while Melvin tried to take it away from him.

"I get to take the maps!" said Henry and Glenn both at the same time. While the boys argued about who would take what, Kate stepped over to the window and picked up the fish bowl. "I get to take Guppy and Whale!" she said.

"No, you don't. I do!" said Tubby, starting toward her, but Kate held the bowl as if she would slosh water in his face if he took another step. He turned back then and began arguing with Nathan about who was to carry the bookends. Miss Jordan settled it by having each of them take one.

Kate poured part of the water from the bowl, and the two fish did not seem to mind. On the way up the trail, she and Ivy discussed Guppy and Whale, who were much calmer than they'd been the day they moved to the hut. Ivy supposed the fish considered themselves experienced travelers by now, or maybe they sensed that they were returning home. Kate thought they were merely relieved that neither of them had been dumped onto the ground again.

Mr. Bronson led the way across the schoolyard and into the building. Partway down the hall he stopped at an open door. "Here we are," he said, motioning for everybody to enter, but no one went inside.

Sylvia said, "But this is the room we had before!"

"Well, yes, so it is."

"But we thought we were getting one of the new rooms."

"I don't know why you thought that," said Mr. Bronson. "The new ones are for the primary grades."

Everyone looked disappointed, and Miss Jordan said, "It's partly my fault. Since the lower grades were already settled, I had thought we'd be given one of the new rooms."

Alex said, "And *I* told everybody we'd have a new room!"

Mr. Bronson asked Alex, "Are you the principal, or am I?"

Instead of answering his father, Alex turned to his classmates. "Let's go back to Hut School."

"Let's do," said Tubby, and everyone began saying yes, that if they weren't to have a new room there was no need to take back the old one.

No one started inside, and Mr. Bronson looked as if he were getting angry. Kate knew there was not a chance of returning to Hut School. "We'll have more space on the playground here," she said. "And we can see the train at recess."

"That's right," said Mr. Bronson. "And it's almost time for the train now."

Nola May said, "But we've already had recess."

Mr. Bronson laughed. "Surely you wouldn't mind having another one. If you'll put your things inside, you may go to the playground now."

The students moved into the room then and began settling into the places where they had sat during the first days of school. Then they went outside, but the train was late and did not pull into the station until recess was over.

Miss Jordan began lessons as soon as everyone was back in the room. First was a discussion of world news. Holding up the front page of the morning's *Atlanta Constitution,* she told the class about comments that had been made by Winston Churchill, Prime Minister of Great Britain. "He's warning us and the British not to start thinking we've almost won the war. In fact, he cautions us against the hopes of an early peace and says that next year our sacrifice of life will be the greatest yet. He says that battles far larger and more costly than Waterloo or Gettysburg will be fought."

"I was hoping the war would be over this year," said Nola May.

"We all wish it would," said Miss Jordan, "and that's what Mr. Churchill is talking about. Here, I'll read you one of his comments. 'There is danger in anything which diverts the thoughts and efforts of any of the Allied Nations from the supreme task which lies before them, namely, that of beating down into dust and ruin the deadly foes and tyrants who so nearly subjugated the entire world to their domination.' "

"What does *subjugated* mean?" asked Alex.

"It means to conquer or bring under complete control." She talked more about Churchill's comments, and it scared Kate to hear that the whole world had almost been conquered. Next, instead of the history lesson that had been planned, Miss Jordan talked about the battles of Waterloo and Gettysburg, and it gave Kate a sick feeling that next year there might be battles that were even worse.

Miss Jordan kept the class so busy for the rest of the day that the misunderstanding about the room was not mentioned again until almost time for the final bell. Henry said, "We were cheated!" and his classmates agreed with him. But the next day their anger was forgotten. It was a day for celebrating. Zack and Tootie had returned to school.

Although he had seen some of his friends every week since he had been away, Zack sounded as if he had been completely out of touch with them. "Have we missed anything?" he asked.

"Not a thing," said Henry. "Nothing ever happens at school."

Miss Jordan laughed. "Why, yes, Zack," she said, "you and Tootie have missed quite a lot. But if you'll work as hard on your studies during the weeks ahead as you have on the farm recently, I'm sure you'll catch up." Early in the afternoon she assigned work to her other students and said that if they would stay busy on their own, she would help Zack and Tootie. "I'll get them started this week," she said, "then they'll be able to go on without me. And maybe this would be a good time for me to say that all of you will be getting along without me soon."

"Without you?" said Tootie, almost shouting it.

Miss Jordan looked sad, thought Kate. *What if she has something terrible like Mrs. Pinson and seems all right now but will go to the hospital and die?*

"I'm going to be leaving," continued Miss Jordan.

"Oh, no!" sighed Winnie; and everybody began exclaiming, "Don't leave!" and "Please stay!"

Kate asked, "Are you sick?"

"No," said Miss Jordan, and Kate felt better. *But what if she's been fired?*

"No, I'm not sick, and I haven't been fired," said Miss Jordan almost as if Kate had asked her question aloud. "However, some fault has been found with my way of teaching, and certainly I'm far from perfect."

Dudley spoke up, "We like your way of teaching."

"Well, thank you," said Miss Jordan. "Maybe some day more people will feel that it's possible to learn and have fun at the same time, but I'm afraid that today such views are not popular. Even so I'd stick around and fight for them if these were ordinary times. But, of course, these are not ordinary times. There's a war on, and I'm so anxious for it to end that I'm enlisting in military service."

"The WACS?" asked Winnie.

"No, the WAVES. I'm joining the Navy instead of the Army."

"Will you help get the war over?" asked Nola May.

Miss Jordan smiled. "Well, I don't know that my going into service will put an end to the war, but maybe if enough women volunteer it will be a help."

Tootie said, "Maybe it's like everybody helping us pick cotton. We got the job done quicker than we ever have."

Alice said, "I think I'll join the WAVES when I get big enough."

"Me too," said Louise, who was echoed by half the girls in the room.

"I'm going to be an Army nurse," said Hope. "I have a cousin who's an Army nurse."

"You have a cousin who's everything!" said Oscar.

Dinah Myrtle said, "Miss Jordan, I don't think I'll be a nurse on account of Veronica Lake."

"Veronica Lake?" said Miss Jordan.

"Yes, ma'am," said Dinah Myrtle, fluffing up a lock of hair that almost covered one of her eyes. "You know, she's the actress who wears her hair like mine."

"Yes," said Miss Jordan. "I know who she is, but not why she would keep you from being a nurse."

"Well, in a picture show called *So Proudly We Hail*, even though she didn't have her hair exactly the way she and I usually fix ours, she was a nurse. And in the end she took a hand grenade and put it inside her dress and walked out into a bunch of enemy soldiers and killed them and her."

"Well, Paulette Goddard and Claudette Colbert got away," said Hope, talking about two other actresses who had been in the movie. "I still want to be an Army nurse."

Miss Jordan said, "Surely the war will be over long before any of you are big enough to get into it."

Zack said, "I'm big enough; I'm just not old enough!"

Miss Jordan laughed. "Oh, yes, I keep forgetting! And if you went in Zack, you'd be a hero. In the meantime you're my hero. All of you are my heroes, my wartime home-front heroes."

Kate asked, "When will you be leaving, Miss Jordan?"

"As soon as my replacement can be found. I've promised to wait until then."

"Good!" said Kate. "Maybe that will take a long time."

"The rest of the year!" said Alice.

"No, I'm sure it will be much sooner than that. I told Mr. Bronson my plans several weeks ago."

"What if the WAVES don't want you?" asked Hope. "I have a cousin—" and before Oscar could say anything, she added, "*another* cousin who couldn't get in."

"I'll be accepted," said Miss Jordan. "I've passed the examinations."

Examinations, thought Kate. They were the tests that had once been mentioned. She was glad Miss Jordan didn't have some terrible illness. And she didn't blame her for going into service if that's what she wanted to do. Kate realized that she herself would probably have done the same thing. Still Kate liked Miss Jordan better than any teacher she had ever had, and that evening she told her father, "Nothing ever stays the way it should. Why can't the good things last?"

"What do you mean?" asked her father.

"Well, whenever anything's going along all right, something always comes along to change it. Like yesterday we didn't mind going back to the main building, but then when we got there we got our old room back instead of a new one. Then today we were happy because Zack and Tootie were in school again, but this afternoon Miss Jordan told us she was leaving. So we didn't stay happy long."

Mrs. Coleman said, "Maybe we appreciate our blessings more when we have disappointments to compare them with."

"It's a poor way to learn a lesson," said Mr. Coleman. "I agree with Kate. Why can't the good things last?"

The
Getaway

By Wednesday, November 17, the sixth grade had been back in the main building a week. It seemed as if they had never left it. "It's almost as if Hut School didn't really happen," said Alice. She was talking to Kate, in line next to her, as they returned from the playground after lunch.

Miss Dillman screamed from the top step, "I said NO TALKING"; and when Kate and Alice passed her, she hissed, "Another word and I'll send you to the office too!" She had sent Zack and Glenn to Mr. Bronson a few minutes earlier when they had started wrestling. Miss Jordan would have separated them, Kate knew, and let it go at that, but she was not there. After returning from lunch she had gone inside, at Mr. Bronson's request, to help another teacher sort out books that had been given to the school. And Miss Dillman had taken charge of all the students on the playground. Why couldn't Miss Dillman have been the one to help sort out books, wondered Kate. It was an aggravation anyway that the sixth and seventh grades had gone back to having lunch and recess together. There seemed no way of getting away from Miss Dillman.

In the afternoon at almost time for the final bell, Miss Jordan said, "Let's close our books now and take a few minutes to chat. I have something to tell you. Your new teacher will be here tomorrow."

"Tomorrow!" said Dudley and Henry at the same time.

"What's she like?" asked Tootie.

"Well, I'm sure she'll be someone you'll enjoy."

"Is she old?" asked Zack.

"No, she's young. She finished college at the end of the summer, but because of sickness in her family she wasn't able to start teaching until now. I have a feeling you're going to like her."

"We'd rather have you," said Alice. "Won't you stay, please?"

"Yes, do!" said Winnie and Kate; and all the girls began pleading.

"Thank you," said Miss Jordan. "I can't stay, but I know you'll be happy with your new teacher, and I hope you'll help her get off to a good start."

"We will," promised the class.

"You can count on us," said Dudley.

"Don't worry about anything!" said Zack, standing up and shaking his fist at the class. "If anybody gives her trouble, they'll have to deal with me!"

Miss Jordan asked, "And what about you? You won't give her any trouble, will you, Zack?"

"Who, me?" asked Zack. "I never give anybody any trouble." Then he added, "Except maybe Glenn."

Everybody laughed, and Miss Jordan pretended to be shocked. "How can the world find peace when two boys can't get along?"

"We'll get along," said Glenn.

"Yes, we'll behave for Miss Whatever-her-name-is," agreed Zack.

"*Miss Edison*," said Miss Jordan. "That's what her name is."

"How long will you stay after she gets here?" asked Dinah Myrtle.

"You don't need two teachers. I'll be finished as soon as the bell rings."

Everyone was silent. Then Miss Jordan smiled. "Come on," she said, "cheer up! You've known I'd be leaving when my replacement came." Just then the bell rang. "So this is good-by. I'll miss you. I'll miss all of you."

"We'll miss you," said Ivy, and everyone began saying good-by.

"Hurry now, don't anyone miss a bus on my account," said Miss Jordan. "Good-by again."

At supper Kate complained to her parents, "Why does it have to be Miss Jordan who's leaving? Of all the teachers, why does she have to be the one?"

"We can't tie strings onto people we love," said her mother.

"You might try it," said Mr. Coleman. "Tie a string to me and see if you can keep me home!" He laughed as if he'd made a good joke, but Mrs. Coleman didn't.

"Have some French fries," she said, "and pass them to Kate. And nobody's said a word about tonight's menu. There's not a dish on the table that's on your list of things you don't like! How's that for cooperation on my part?"

"You get A plus," said Mr. Coleman. "Unless of course there's no dessert!"

"There's a war on!" said Kate.

"Even so," said Mrs. Coleman, "we're having dessert tonight!" And a few minutes later she brought out a cherry pie.

"Is this a special occasion?" asked Kate.

Her parents looked at each other. "Let's just call it *an occasion*," said Mr. Coleman; and Mrs. Coleman said, "I felt that we needed to be cheered up!" Kate had a feeling that something was happening that she was not being told about, but with cherry pie in front of her it was not easy to think about anything else. And as soon as the pie was finished and the dishes washed, it was time for "Kay Kyser's College of Musical Knowledge" on the radio. Maybe Ish Kabibble would say a funny poem.

Miss Edison was at school the next day. She was taller than Miss Jordan and had red hair. "She's got glamour," whispered Dinah Myrtle.

"Like you and Veronica Lake?" asked Glenn.

"No," said Dinah Myrtle. "She's more like Rita Hayworth."

At recess the sixth graders gathered together at the end of the playground. It was as far from Miss Dillman and her grade as they could get. Also it was across from the depot, and the train was due.

"What would you like to play?" asked Miss Edison.

Henry said, "What about Simon Says?" and everyone laughed, including Miss Edison.

"I have an idea you're pulling my leg," she said, "but all right, we'll play Simon Says! Everybody get in front of me, and I'll be Simon." But after the students had arranged themselves in front of her, she said, "Maybe one of you should be Simon. Kate, I appoint you to take my place."

Kate, pleased that Miss Edison knew her name already, stepped to the front. She noticed a big group of men in the depot yard and realized that this was Thursday, the day draftees were sent to Fort McPherson for examinations. Then she saw a woman standing by a suitcase. "Say," she said, "there's Miss Jordan!" and everybody looked toward the depot. Kate said, "Quick, now, everybody, crouch like you're set to run a race."

Nobody crouched, and Kate yelled, "I mean, Simon says to crouch."

At that her classmates crouched as if they were toeing a line. Dudley grinned at Kate, and she knew that he had guessed what her next command would be. "Hurry!" he called, and Kate gave the signal. "Simon says for all of us to run over and see Miss Jordan off!" At that, all the boys and girls hurried toward the depot yard. Miss Edison did not yell for them to come back, but she did call, "Be careful crossing the road!"

The train pulled into the station just as they got there. Most of the girls began hugging Miss Jordan, saying how much they'd miss her and how they hated to see her leave.

Mr. Wilson, the conductor, put down a platform at the entrance to one of the day coaches, and the crowd began moving toward it. At the same time, the depot agent and his helper rushed about, loading mailbags and freight, and Mrs. Dixon, the secretary of the draft board, called out instructions to three draftees who had arrived late. "Mr. Rogers has your tickets," she said.

While so many things were happening, Kate had an idea. She whispered it to Dudley, "Let's run climb onto the back of the train and ride to Two-Mile Crossing with Miss Jordan. Mr. Wilson won't mind."

Instantly the word spread among the boys, and soon all of them

and Kate had climbed aboard the observation platform of the last car, and seconds later the train pulled out of the station. Mr. Wilson appeared back of them just as it started past the schoolyard. They could hear one of the draftees calling to Miss Edison, "Hey, teacher, I wish I went to school!" and another yelled, "What about giving *me* a lesson?"

Then Miss Dillman saw Kate and the boys. "Stop the train!" she screamed. "Get those children off!"

Mr. Wilson waved at her. "Gotta get a load of draftees to the city!" he answered. "It's my patriotic duty!"

All the boys and Kate laughed, and then Mr. Wilson called to Miss Dillman and Miss Edison, "We'll stop at Two-Mile Crossing and send them back!"

Everybody aboard was laughing as the train chugged away. Everybody on the school ground, except Miss Dillman, was laughing too.

"Now let's go inside," said Mr. Wilson, "and find places for you near that pretty little teacher who's going away."

Most of the people who had boarded the train in Redhill were seated in one car. At the back of it, Melvin asked Kate, "Ain't that your father up there?" He was looking toward the man sitting directly in back of Miss Jordan.

"It sure is!" said Kate; and when they reached him, she said, "I didn't know you were going to Atlanta today?"

Mr. Coleman laughed. "I didn't know you were either!"

"We're just going as far as Two-Mile Crossing. It's sort of a send-off for Miss Jordan."

Miss Jordan asked, "What will your new teacher think?"

"She'll understand," said Dudley.

"I was right about her, wasn't I?" said Miss Jordan. "I'm so glad to be leaving you in good hands."

By then Mr. Wilson, who had stopped near the back of the car, caught up with the group. He asked Mr. Coleman, "Do you have the tickets for all of you?"

Kate thought he was asking if her father had tickets for her and the boys, but Mr. Coleman said, "No, I believe Mrs. Dickson gave our tickets to Ben Rogers."

A man on the front seat called, "Yes, I've got the tickets." He held up a large envelope, and Kate saw the lettering on the back of it: SELECTIVE SERVICE. Suddenly she realized that her father was one of the draftees. She looked at him, and for a brief moment he was not smiling. Then Kate asked, "Why didn't you tell me?"

"Well, after I take the tests, I'll have three weeks to get matters settled at home. I thought there'd be plenty of time then."

Mr. Wilson said, "I didn't realize I was giving away military secrets when I asked about the tickets."

"She'd have found out soon," answered Mr. Coleman. Then he turned to Kate. "How about it? Uncle Sam wants me in the war!"

Kate said, "But you can't shoot!" and everyone sitting nearby laughed.

Her father said, "I wonder if Robert E. Lee's daughter said, 'But you can't shoot!' when he went off to win his war!"

A man across the aisle, another of the draftees, said, "Maybe he couldn't shoot; maybe that's why the South lost the war!"

The man beside him said, "But we'll win this one! We're fighting with the Yankees instead of against them now, and ain't nothing can stop us!"

"You tell 'em!" shouted a man in the back, and another yelled "Yah-hoo!" Soon everyone was laughing and talking. The draftees made wisecracks about who would prove the most heroic in battle, and Kate thought of her mother's comment about men going off to

war as if the whole thing were a big lark. Then she thought of
Marcus Holbrook. The war had not been a lark for him. And
what about the blind man at the hospital, the one who had been a
commercial artist before he went in service? And the amputees? It
had not been a lark for any of them, and Kate wanted to scream
out, "Some of you will get your guts shot out a long way from
home." Hadn't her father once said this? "Some of you ain't never
coming back, do you hear?" But she didn't say these things; and
the men went on making jokes. Kate knew they weren't as happy
as they pretended to be. There was a look in the eyes of each of
them that was not carefree, in spite of all the laughter. She re-
called her father saying, "We all have to put up a front at times."

Even Miss Jordan acted now as if the war were an exciting
game. "We'll win before you get out of the sixth grade!" she said
to Kate and the boys.

"We'll win before Christmas!" said a man in overalls seated in
front of her.

"Before Thanksgiving!" said the man beside him.

"It wouldn't surprise me if the war didn't end this afternoon!"
said Ben Rogers. "When Hitler hears we're coming, he'll give up!"

The jokes, the exaggeration, and the air of confidence covered
up uncertainty and fear, Kate knew, and by the time the train
pulled to a stop at Two-Mile Crossing, she was laughing with
everyone else. When Mr. Wilson took her hand for the long step
to the ground, he said, "Now don't any of you try another stunt
like this, or we'll be in trouble." Then he smiled and added, "But
it's O.K. this time. After all, there's a war on!"

The boys and Kate stood by the roadside and watched the train
gather speed.

Kate waved at her father and Miss Jordan and wished nothing

had changed from the way it had been a month ago—or the month before that. But if nothing ever changed, the war would never end, and she reminded herself, nothing stays the same forever, the good or the bad. Aloud she said, "But why can't the good things last?"

Everyone looked at her, and Dudley asked, "What did you say?"

"I said I'll beat you back to town," said Kate, and before the boys could realize a race was underway she was far ahead of them.

About the Author

ROBERT BURCH was born in Fayette County, Georgia, and grew up there with seven brothers and sisters. Despite the economic hardships of the nineteen thirties, he relishes many happy memories of those years. Mr. Burch draws on his childhood experiences for background material in his books, but, he says, "the incidents come from my imagination." Georgia is the setting for many of his popular books for young people, including *Queenie Peavy,* an ALA Notable Book, *Renfroe's Christmas,* and *Doodle and the Go-cart.*

Robert Burch now lives in the house in which he spent his youth. He is a frequent lecturer at book fairs and conventions, but devotes most of his time to writing—the career he says he "would not trade for any other."